Baz knows that h̶̶̶̶̶̶ ̶̶̶̶̶̶̶̶̶ ̶̶̶̶̶̶̶̶̶ been proud of him, if only he'd b̶e̶e̶n̶ around to see. He's just won a scholarship to Bryce's, the poshest school in town.

But he quickly learns that it takes more than a scholarship to be accepted at this place and he's soon in trouble for protecting the juniors when they get bullied, for questioning all the petty rules and regulations and for objecting when the school buys some building land for yet more tennis-courts, putting his best friend's dad out of a job.

When Bryce's lets its pupils have a school election, to coincide with the national one, Baz forms his own party, to fight for what he believes in. Plump, loyal Alice and beautiful Vanessa stick up for him, as does clever 'Polly' Pollitt and crazy Jake Elder. But the snobbish Julius Malin with his Cut Above supporters does all he can to crush him. So do some of the teachers who fear that nothing but 'wildness' and 'unruly behaviour' will come out of his radical Common Man party.

Ann Pilling was brought up in industrial Lancashire where many of her books are set, but has also lived in Wales, London, Buckinghamshire and on the east and west coasts of the USA. For some years she taught English, but has been writing since 1979. She now lives in Oxford with her husband, her two sons and a tortoiseshell cat called Victoria. She likes singing, cooking, music, gardening and walking in the Yorkshire Dales, to which she retreats whenever possible.

ANN PILLING

Vote for Baz

(Fanfare for the Common Man)

PUFFIN BOOKS

PUFFIN BOOKS

Published by the Penguin Group
Penguin Books Ltd, 27 Wrights Lane, London W8 5TZ, England
Penguin Books USA Inc., 375 Hudson Street, New York, New York 10014, USA
Penguin Books Australia Ltd, Ringwood, Victoria, Australia
Penguin Books Canada Ltd, 10 Alcorn Avenue, Toronto, Ontario, Canada M4V 3B2
Penguin Books (NZ) Ltd, 182–190 Wairau Road, Auckland 10, New Zealand

Penguin Books Ltd, Registered Offices: Harmondsworth, Middlesex, England

First published by Viking 1992
Published in Puffin Books 1993
1 3 5 7 9 10 8 6 4 2

Text copyright © Ann Pilling, 1992
All rights reserved

The moral right of the author has been asserted

Printed in England by Clays Ltd, St Ives plc
Filmset in Monophoto Palatino

For Porter

1

Baz was having trouble with his left ear-lobe. The first ear-ring had gone in like a dream; he'd got the knack now and he'd not even had to look in the bathroom mirror. But his second ear was being difficult, as usual. The hairdresser who'd pierced them for him had said he'd have no problems, just so long as he kept the little gold blobby things in at night. They made sure the holes stayed open until your ears got used to it. But while he was asleep some skin must have grown over his left hole again. It *must* have.

As he fiddled he heard the letter-box click, and a faint plop as something landed on the mat. His heart did a little flip and he got a touch of that sickly, nervous feeling he'd had two months ago, when he'd done the exam. *Today was the day.* His future was downstairs, lying against the door in an envelope, a fat white one if he'd passed, a thin brown one if he'd failed. *Ugh.* The sickly feeling got worse and he started to tidy up the bathroom, breathing on the mirror and making a great business of studying his appearance. He couldn't go down and pick up the post, not yet. He daren't.

He rubbed a circle clear in the steamy glass and looked at himself. He really was rather handsome, he decided, a perfect mix of Mum and Dad; he had Mum's straight nose and high cheek-bones, Dad's height and long, easy limbs, his mass of tight black curls. His skin was medium coffee, a 50/50 blend. Dad's family had been here for generations, but way back they'd been African. He'd been in the middle of making a family tree when ... *No.* Baz couldn't think about his father this morning.

He stared harder into the circle of glass and ran his fingers over his head. He definitely needed a haircut. It was getting to be an Afro and Afros weren't allowed at school, not even when you had the proper sort of hair like him. It was in the rules. What sort of rules would they have at Bryce's?

Slowly, almost counting between the individual treads, he descended the stairs, his eyes focusing on the doormat and its bundle of letters, fastened together with a green rubber band. Suddenly he didn't want to go through this next bit on his own, he wanted his father with him.

Dad. Just how tall had he been? Had he had funny drooping ear-lobes, like Baz? And a peculiar big toe that stuck out a bit from the others? It was awful, he couldn't remember. At this moment he couldn't even remember his *face*. That's what came of not talking to people about what had happened two years ago; but he couldn't help it. He swept up the packet of mail and went through to the back with it.

Bills, more bills, a magazine for his mother, and something telling them they could win a new Toyota in a competition. Then The Letter, long, white and fat with some Latin on the back, and the crest of Bryce's school. But it was addressed to Mrs Helen Bradshaw, 17 Inkerman Street, Darnley-in-Makerfield, and she got cross if he opened her letters, *so* . . . Baz felt it all over, sniffed at it, held it up to the light. Then, with massive self-control, he propped it against his mother's coffee mug, poured out cornflakes for himself and began reading about the Toyota competition.

He chewed his breakfast without enthusiasm, looking across at the fat white envelope between every second mouthful. Then he picked it up again to see if the contents slid from one end to the other. After all, it might only contain a rejection slip. They could have run out of cheap brown ones and be using these posh envelopes for everybody.

'Oh . . .' Baz was jigging up and down with frustration now, making a peevish urgent sound like a toddler who needs to go somewhere. It was no good, he *couldn't* wait. Mum ought to be in by now, something must have delayed her at work.

She'd understand if he opened her letter. It should have been addressed to *him*, anyhow. With a thumping heart he reached across the table, picked up the breadknife and slit the envelope open with shaking fingers.

'I am pleased to inform you,' he read, 'that in the recent scholarship examinations your son, Basil William Bradshaw, gained an average mark of 87%, and that we are pleased to offer him . . .' There was a lot more, and a great wadge of printed stuff about uniform, sport, and parent–teacher activities. But Baz didn't need to look at anything else. He repacked the envelope, propped it in place against Mum's mug and poured out more cornflakes. He was suddenly very hungry now, it must be the sheer relief. He concentrated hard on eating as he listened for the sound of a key in the back-door lock. But inside he was giving great whoops of joy. 87 per cent! He'd *done* it!

When Mum heard she smiled, properly, for the first time since Dad. Then she hugged Baz so hard he very nearly threw up, bringing back all the cornflakes. Then she grabbed him and led him round the kitchen in a kind of war-dance. 'I knew you'd do it, I *knew*,' she shouted, half laughing, half crying.

'No you didn't, you said not to count my chickens. I remember. You told me not to be big-headed . . . Listen, Mum, can we sit down? I'm feeling sick.'

These days they didn't hug and kiss very much. Baz got too embarrassed. But he could tell that his mother was reluctant to let him go. She was sitting at the table now but she still kept leaning across and touching his face in a kind of wonder. He knew what she was thinking, that he looked like his father. 'Too much', he'd heard her tell Billie, the funny little friend she'd made at the Widows' Club.

He said, 'There's a lot of stuff about uniform.'

'I know.' She was looking at all the lists. 'This is going to cost a bomb, Baz . . . but they *do* have a second-hand sale. That'll help.'

Second-hand? He didn't fancy that. His mother worked very hard at her various jobs. She did office cleaning before breakfast and she also had several old people to look after. She wasn't paid all that much, but she kept them both looking smart.

'Let's have a look at it, then,' he said, reaching over for the clothing list. 'Regulation grey flannels, regulation blazer with regulation badge . . . heck Mum, it's all rules and regulations . . .' He read on. 'And look at this: regulation *shoes*. What are they, when they're at home?'

'Search me. But Bryce's pupils always look smart, Baz, that's the point. Now let's see . . .' She'd already got her pocket calculator out and was adding up figures.

In the hall the phone rang. She got up and clicked her teeth. 'Damn. I wanted to phone Billie, to tell her the news. Hope it's not Mrs Iveson, from Fifty Nine. You know how she goes on and on.'

Baz felt sad when he thought about Mum enthusiastically phoning Billie. Of course he was glad she'd *got* a special friend, and he was glad it wasn't a man. He'd thought it was when he'd heard the name, but Billie's real name was Mary. He just wished they'd got some family to tell his great news to, family, like other people. Everyone he knew had got aunties, grannies and things; not the Bradshaws though.

Mum said it was because she and Dad had both been 'only' children, so there couldn't be any uncles and aunts and cousins, could there? And Dad's parents had died years ago when Baz was a baby. But Mum had parents, in the South, where she had come from, yet Baz didn't even know them. They'd not wanted her to marry Dad; they'd said if she did she was 'no daughter of ours'. They'd said disgusting things about black people. When the thing happened to Dad, Mum's father, Mr Scotson, had written a letter saying they would come and see her. She'd screwed it up. It was far too late for all that, she had said bitterly.

'That was Mrs Sugden,' she told him, coming back to the

4

table and slotting more bread in the toaster. 'Alice has got in too. Isn't that great?'

'What did she get?'

'83 per cent.'

He must have looked a bit pleased because his mother leaned over and poked him. 'Don't *gloat*, just because you beat her by a few marks. She's got *in*, that's the point. She's got into Bryce's and her mother's over the moon.'

Baz sniggered. Alice's mother was enormous. She went to Weight Watchers with her fat friend, Dorothy. He saw them waddling down Inkerman Street most Tuesday nights. The Sugdens lived at the top, the posh end, in the newer semi-detached houses. Baz and his mum lived in a terrace near the bottom. 'Hey diddle diddle the cat and the fiddle/The cow jumped over the moon,' he hummed quietly.

'What? What's that?' His mother was studying the grand total on her calculator. 'I'll tell you something Baz, if we buy everything on this list we'll have to take out a mortgage.'

'Does it say anything about jewellery?'

'Jewellery? No, I'm sure it doesn't . . . no, nothing.'

'Well, do you think I'll be allowed to wear my ear-rings, then?'

Mrs Bradshaw was aghast. 'At Bryce's? *Ear-rings*? Are you mad?'

'You wear them.'

'Listen, sunshine, we've been through all this before, that's different.'

'I don't see how,' Baz said stubbornly.

'Well you know it is. I didn't want you to get yours done in the first place.'

'But, Mum, loads of people do and, anyhow, school doesn't mind, so long as you are neat and tidy. That's what Mr Greaves told us. I like him, he's great. Bet *he* wore them when he was my age.'

'Hmm, maybe he did. But can you imagine the headmaster of Bryce's with a couple of curtain-rings in his ears? I mean,

5

you've seen him, honey. Now don't be difficult. What does it matter?'

'It *does* matter, Mum, of course it matters, it's a question of human freedom.'

Mrs Bradshaw opened her mouth and then shut it again. The piercing of Baz's ears, strictly against orders, had caused a big row. As she turned her back and ran water into the sink to wash up, he thought she muttered something like 'just like your father'.

'What? *What?*'

'I was just thinking it would be nice if you and Alice went on the bus together, to Bryce's. She won't know anyone either. You can be new together.'

'Aw Mum, not *Alice*. Everyone'll laugh.'

Alice Sugden was OK, but she was fat like her mother, and people stared at her in the street. Really she ought to go to Weight Watchers too. Furthermore, Baz suspected she might have a bit of a crush on him. When he used to go to their house for piano lessons she always acted a bit funny when she let him into the front room. You could tell when girls fancied you.

He wasn't having piano lessons at the moment, Mum had a cash-flow problem; but when the compensation came through from Dad's company she'd promised they would start up again. Secretly he didn't much mind if they didn't. Mrs Sugden made him play boring little pieces and her great bosoms embarrassed him. When she leaned over to show him the proper fingering for things, they nearly touched the piano keys. He reckoned she could play great crashing chords with them.

He said, 'I'll be going to Bryce's with Kev, Mum, we've fixed it.'

Mrs Bradshaw gave a watery little smile. She didn't approve of Baz's friendship with Kevin White, the boy next door. Kevin was the author of the ear-rings, and generally scruffy. His latest fashion move was to stop washing his

hair. 'Oh, has he got in too, then?' she said without enthusiasm.

'Well, yeah, he's bound to have passed if Alice has.'

But then it occurred to Baz that Kev hadn't actually been
round with his acceptance letter, and a doubt struck him.
'Mum, can I go and see?'

'OK. Don't be long though. You've got to leave for school
in ten minutes.' She got up. 'I'm going to phone Billie before
she goes to work. She'll be thrilled. I think we should have a
little celebration tonight.'

Baz didn't need to ask whether Kev had got into Bryce's.
The thick, gloomy atmosphere hit him as soon as he opened
the kitchen door. The Whites' was always a bit of a tip, but
the house seemed worse than usual, with great piles of
unwashed dishes toppling over in the sink, a load of dirty
washing dumped in a corner and something that looked like
old baked beans stuck to the front of the cooker in a foul
glob. Kev was still in his pyjamas sitting in front of the television.

Baz moved some of the washing and perched on a corner of
the grubby settee. Kev's house always depressed him, it had a
funny smell. When they argued, which wasn't very often, Kev
usually ended up by going on about Baz's mother being
fanatical about cleaning her house. He said it wasn't natural.
But the Bradshaws couldn't function in a tip like this and,
anyhow, Baz didn't mind having to keep his room tidy or
about doing his jobs. He did worry a bit about his mother.
Now she didn't have Dad she *was* getting a bit too keen on
washing and scrubbing. Sometimes he heard her Hoovering in
the middle of the night.

He'd told Kev it worried him. Sometimes they talked
about their private family things together, but only when
they were both in the mood; about what had happened to
Baz's dad, and about Kev's mother clearing off to Newcastle.
They understood each other very well. Kev seemed to know

when Baz couldn't face any questions about the Dad episode and Baz knew when Kev had had it about his parents splitting up. When other people got too nosy they closed ranks and protected each other. It was really how they'd become friends.

Kev's dad had gone in the opposite direction from Mrs Bradshaw after the split, and their house had always been a mess. They'd only moved next door a year ago, when Mrs White went off. She lived in Newcastle now with a 50-year-old boyfriend called Max, and she'd just had a baby. Kev had refused to go to Newcastle and they'd sold their big house in Denning on the other side of town, split the cash between them and moved in here. It was going to be a 'new start' for Kev and his father. Getting into Bryce's was going to be part of it. But he hadn't got in. Baz could see the letter lying on the rug in front of the gas fire. He could read upside-down quite easily and it started 'We regret'.

He said, 'I don't understand this, Kev.'

'Dry up about it, can't you.' The tone of Kev's voice was quite new, a nasty little snarl. He'd been crying.

'You were a dead cert Kev, everyone said so.'

'It was the maths. I blew the maths. Read it if you don't believe me, the marks are in that,' and Kev nudged the rejection letter across the rug with his foot.

Baz glanced at the three-sentence letter. 'But Alice couldn't do maths and she got in.'

'Ah, but she had all that special coaching didn't she?' Kev said sourly. 'Dad couldn't afford that, not just after the move. Anyhow, who wants to go to Bryce's? It's a snob school.'

'But you took the exam,' Baz said stoutly, his own achievement suddenly threatened now. 'You *did* want to go, Kev, you said. It was the Rugby. That's why you wanted Bryce's. And your Dad, your Dad was dead keen, Kev.'

'Rugby, don't give me that.' Kev pronounced it like some terrible swear word. 'Dad won't be bothered anyhow, he's got a problem at work.'

8

'Can I see the letter?'

'Feel free.' Kev turned up the television very loud and hunched over it, pointedly ignoring Baz. His breath was bad. He'd obviously not cleaned his teeth yet, and his hair had a greasy smell. After the neatness and order of his own home Baz felt depressed by it all. He said, scrutinizing the crumpled sheet, 'I don't think these marks are right, Kev. They *can't* be. I think they are someone else's. Listen, why don't you get your dad to ring up?'

'What's the point? He doesn't care.'

''Course he cares. He was dead keen for you to go to Bryce's, he was as keen as my mum and the Sugdens. Go on Kev, get him to talk to the headmaster. I bet he'd —'

Kev leaned forward, thrust his face close to Baz's and clenched his fists. 'Listen you, *I've not got in.* It says so. Don't you believe plain English?' He was talking to Baz through gritted teeth now, and there was a kind of hate in his voice.

'I don't believe that,' Baz said doggedly. He'd never dreamed he and Kev wouldn't go to Bryce's together.

'Well, you've got to believe it. I'm not going.'

Baz leaned forward and turned the TV down. 'OK. I'm not going either.'

Kev stared at him and his mouth twisted. 'Don't give me that. After all that swotting? You'll go, Basil Bradshaw. Bet you got the top mark too, didn't you? Everyone said you would.'

Baz felt himself blushing. 'Dunno. I think I beat Alice. Listen are you coming to school? It's nearly twenty to.'

'Ne'er. Think I'll skip it today.' And Kev restored the television set to full volume. 'Mind if I get on with my programme?'

It was definitely dismissal, and Baz let himself out of the house with the certain knowledge that something between him and Kev White had snapped. Five minutes later he was striding down the street towards school. It was a brilliant July morning, the long narrow strip of sky between the dingy red-brick terraces was a marvellous blue dazzle and he'd got his place at Bryce's. But the glory had somehow gone out of everything.

2

Normally Baz liked the first day of a new school year: the crisp new mornings after the long stale summer, new shoes, new sports gear, the smell of new pens and pencils in a brand-new bag. Mum always started him off with the proper kit. Today, though, he felt sick with nerves, there had been too much of a build-up about getting this big scholarship to Bryce's. For a start there had been hours of shopping. Mum was fussy and always demanded value for money, so it had taken forever to find exactly what she wanted at exactly the right price. Then there were interminable phone calls to Mrs Sugden comparing notes, and long chats with Billie. Last night they had gone halves down at the Star of Bengal and treated him to a celebration meal. Curry was his favourite thing, but he'd left most of it. It was nerves about Bryce's. Whether people would actually talk to him and what the teachers would be like and whether, when he got there, he'd find that he wasn't clever at all, just ordinary. Whether people would say things about him being coffee colour. Mum said they had all sorts going to Bryce's, that people went there because they were clever.

Kev had been foul to him ever since he'd got the scholarship. Over the summer they hardly spoke. When they did Kev just needled him all the time about going to Bryce's, saying it was a snob school and that you only got there if you paid. Getting a free place through sitting an exam didn't seem to be any different from paying, to him. When Baz had reminded him that he'd sat the exam too, he just walked off.

Mum said Kev's problem was his parents, his mother going off to Newcastle and his father being too fond of the bottle.

Over the summer she'd knocked on the party-wall a couple of times, when his bawling and shouting on his return from the pub had woken them up at night. Mr White had knocked back. It was Kev Baz worried about, but he couldn't get through any more. He missed him badly. Underneath the rough awkwardness he'd found that Kev White was OK.

There he stood in the bus queue, talking to Alex Brodey; they seemed very pally. That was bad news. Alex Brodey was a real tearaway; he spent half his time doing detentions and the other half sitting outside Mr Greaves' door waiting for them. Quite often he didn't go to school at all. The queer thing was that his parents were dead strict, and mega-respectable. Mrs Brodey was a school governor and they were always in the papers fighting local campaigns for things. Mum said that was half the trouble; that they didn't keep their eyes on Alex enough, that he was an only child who had spent too much time on his own. Baz wasn't so sure. He was an only child too. The point was that some people were just plain *bad* and he'd always detested Alex. He had a thin sharp face rather like a weasel and a nasty habit of laughing at other people's misfortunes.

From along the queue the weaselly face was staring at him now, its nasty pointed mouth and chin twisted into its usual sarcastic smile. Then its owner nudged Kev in the ribs and they collapsed into sly giggles. Baz felt his cheeks burning. They were obviously laughing at him, all done up like a dog's dinner in his bottle-green Bryce's uniform with his neatly ironed pale-blue shirt and his green and silver tie. The little boys – and there were several of them in the queue because Bryce's had a junior department – even wore caps. That was ridiculous for a start, in fact *uniform* was ridiculous. That was why, on his way to the bus, he'd stopped and inserted an ear-ring in his right ear. Only a very small one, nothing you'd notice. For all Mum's careful shopping his new trousers felt a bit tight, his shirt was scratchy, he was generally uncomfortable. He turned away from the manic giggles of Kev and Alex and studied the bus queue.

It was divided into two definite camps, solid blocks of neat grey, mixed in with green and silver stripes – that was Bryce's – and the more cheerful motley of the Comprehensive where you could wear what you wanted so long as it wasn't too outlandish, and you were reasonably neat and tidy. That's what Mr Greaves always said about school dress. Some parents, Alex Brodey's among them, had actually asked for uniform, but Mr Greaves had stuck out. His view was that his pupils should try to make their own decisions, make a few mistakes, learn something. Compare that with the six pages of *Rules* that had just come from Bryce's. Baz hadn't even started at the place yet and already he felt doubtful.

One of the little lads in a gigantic green cap was being got at, poked and pulled and pushed into the road by a lanky fair-haired individual in a tweedy coat and black shoes polished up like mirrors. Baz watched him. He must be a senior. You could only tell he was from Bryce's because of the tie. 'Aw, leave off, Julius,' he heard, a thin cheeping voice like the cry of a hopeful fledgling. But 'Julius' was clearly enjoying himself. So was his companion, a handsome chunky boy who looked about Baz's age but who had a figure like a male model, broad shoulders tapering down to a narrow waist, arms and legs in perfect proportion, a real sportsman's physique. Like Baz, he was coffee-coloured and he'd felt a little surge of hope when he first saw him in the queue, but now he didn't like his ugly laughter, nor his bland smile of satisfaction when the enormous green cap splatted into a puddle, to be restored to its immaculately-combed poll by tweedy Julius. 'Aw, *Julius* ...' The little bird-voice was nearly crying now as puddle-water trickled down his face in muddy streaks. Baz's hands itched, wanting to sock both bully-boys in the jaw. He mustn't though. Dumping his new bag on the pavement he made his way along the queue to see Kev.

'How are you doing, then?' It had taken an effort to come up the queue and say that, it had taken forgiveness. But Kev wasn't having any. He was chewing gum. With a sly look at Alex Brodey he blew a great bubble and popped it in Baz's face, then he unrolled a comic from under his arm and started to read. 'I see you *are* going then?' he mumbled, scarcely bothering to open his mouth.

'Going where?'

'Bryce's.'

Baz felt about an inch high. 'Well, yes. Of course I am.'

'Thought you said you *weren't* going, or didn't I hear straight?'

Baz was silent. Of all the stupid things he'd said in his life he knew that his impulsive declaration not to go to Bryce's without Kev was just about the stupidest. He'd said it in a rush of generosity, without thinking, to make Kev feel better the day he'd got his rejection letter. He said, 'Why didn't you get your dad to speak to them?' No answer, and another obscene pink bubble and a rude splat as it exploded.

'Mrs Sugden says he should have, Kev. She said they can make mistakes.'

'*Mrs Sugden* . . .' Kev's voice was poisonous. 'What does she know about anything? And where's her little darling, where's Fat Alice? Thought she'd be first in the queue on her first morning.'

'Dunno. It's a long walk from the other end of Inkerman Street. I suppose she's still on her way.' He felt guilty about Alice. He was supposed to have waited in, to be called for, but while his mother was upstairs he had slipped out. He couldn't face starting his career at Bryce's with Alice clinging round his neck, and that's how it'd be. She was a clinger, and she fancied him.

'Listen, Kev,' he said, 'can you come round after school? We've just bought a video, we could get a film out.'

Kev's eyes definitely kindled. *A video recorder next door at the Bradshaws.* It could mean riches. He was a real telly addict. He was definitely wavering. But then Alex Brodey whispered something in his ear and he muttered, 'No thanks. I'm doing something, for my dad.' And he moved away.

It was a lie and they both knew it was. 'Go on, Kev,' Baz

14

wheedled. Suddenly he felt quite desperate to wean Kev away from the company of Alex Brodey. 'They get the new films in today.'

'I said I'm *doing* things.'

'But Kev . . .'

'Leave off me, can't you, *creep*. Anyhow, what are you doing here, pushing into the queue?'

'I'm not, I'm not. My bag's up there.'

'Better go and be reunited with it then, hadn't you?' and he popped his third and biggest bubble so far.

'You new too then?'

'Yes.' The handsome black boy who'd helped push the little lad into the gutter eyed Baz coldly. His uniform was immaculate, fitting so beautifully he might have been sewn into it and his crisp shirt was dazzling white against his coffee skin. Baz could smell the rich tang of the new olde-worlde leather 'satchel' which was slung casually from one shoulder. Bags like that cost big money and they were coming back into fashion. His own bag, a bright-red canvas holdall with a banana design, suddenly looked tawdry and cheap. He wished he'd not stencilled. 'I'm bananas about Liverpool' on it, last night. It didn't seem such a brilliant joke now, and bags like this were probably against The Rules.

'Where do you live?' Baz asked him.

There was no reply but he thought the other boy had edged away from him slightly, wrinkling his nose as if he'd smelt a bad smell.

'We live on Inkerman Street, me and Alice Sugden. We've both won scholarships. Have you?'

It was definitely the wrong thing to say. Baz had meant it to be flattering, after all, only clever people got scholarships to Bryce's, but the boy didn't like it. He said, 'I'm only here until the summer, I started last term. My father has been posted abroad. Darnley-in-Makerfield's not my home.' His accent was cut glass, the kind you heard on the radio when

15

they were taking off Prince Charles, and he pronounced 'Darn-ley' as if it were a public lavatory, as if the only good thing about it was the railway station, where you could get trains to take you out of the place.

'But where do you *live*?' persisted Baz.

'In Denning, with my aunt and uncle, on Palace Road.'

Baz brightened. Denning, with its rambling Victorian houses and leafy gardens, was the most 'desirable' part of the town. And he too had friends in Denning. *Had had*. Kev had lived there before his mother had crashed off to Newcastle with slimy Max Fenton.

'Well, as I say,' he said chattily, determined to be friendly, 'we live on Inkerman Street. Do you know it at all? The houses are quite old. It's near the slipper factory. Bit of a walk to the bus, but still . . . the reason it's called Inkerman . . .'

'I don't know it.' The boy was turning his back. Then he said out of the corner of his mouth, 'What does your father do then, make slippers?'

Next to him Bully Julius snorted with laughter. And from up the queue Alex Brodey yelled, 'Baz Bradshaw's not *got* a father.' The sneak must have been listening.

Baz, in real terror in case the boy from Denning should ask about Dad, dropped his banana bag in confusion. Julius picked it up and handed it to him. 'Hmm,' he muttered, inspecting the design, 'Bananas . . . it'd look good in the jungle.' At his side the Denning boy sniggered and suddenly Baz hated them both. They were in this together, whatever it was, this sneery do-you-down thing. 'I'm not sure Slime would approve though,' Julius went on authoritatively, 'and I'd take that ear-ring out if I were you.'

'Why? The rules don't mention jewellery,' Baz said, suddenly belligerent. He was fed up of these rude unfriendly people, fed up of Kev and Alex, fed up of Bryce's, and he'd not even got to the place yet.

'They don't need to, my friend. I can tell you, Slime will be down on you like a ton of bricks if he sees that. Take it out now if you want my advice.'

16

'I don't particularly,' and Baz stared at the arrogant boy in tweed, the arrogant Julius. 'Who's Slime, anyhow?'

'Slime's the headmaster, and he's definitely not a man to cross, especially when you are new. Suit yourself, if you want to get into trouble,' and he turned away as the bus drew up. The queue surged forwards and everybody piled in.

As it moved out into the road, Baz, from an upstairs window, saw Alice puffing along the pavement, yelling, 'Stop! Wait for me, *please* . . .' as if anybody would take any notice. He thought she looked grotesque stuffed into her green Bryce's uniform. Her grey pleated skirt was much too short and showed her thick tube-like hockey legs to hideous disadvantage; somehow her tie had got wrapped round her neck and looked as though it was choking her, she was so red in the face.

As she reached the bus-stop she caught her foot in a great crack in the paving and fell over. It was famous that crack. Alex Brodey's parents had campaigned about it, in one of their protests. They'd always said it would cause a nasty accident and that the local authority would be liable. Now it had.

'Oops,' giggled Julius to the black boy from Denning. 'Oops, I can see her knickers!'

So could Baz, they were green to match her uniform, and there was quite a lot of them.

'Your friend is she?' the Denning boy drawled. 'The other scholarship winner from Slipper Street?'

'It's Inkerman Street actually and, yes, she's been my friend for years and years,' Baz said, in a sudden fierceness of loyalty, and the bus rumbled off, leaving Fat Alice weeping on the pavement.

3

Bryce's and Darnley Comprehensive were next door to each other, on rising ground to the west side of Stockport New Road. As if in recognition of the fact that the two schools were equal in importance, the communal bus-stop was situated exactly half-way between the properties, which were separated from each other by a long strip of fence behind which stretched a mysterious, heavily-wooded piece of overgrown waste land called Pullen's Field.

It was mysterious because for years nobody seemed to know who owned it. There wasn't much spare land in Darnley, you had to go up on the moors for space and fresh air, so any bit of green attracted the locals like flies to the jam pot. Baz had played on Pullen's Field once. He remembered building dens there, and climbing the trees. But then the fences had been put up and high gates with padlocks but still nothing happened to it, it just *was*, all bolted and barred, no use to anybody.

Now, though, something was obviously happening. As he got off the bus he spotted a notice on posts behind the fence: 'E. Ridgeway and Sons, Building Contractors'. He stared at it, dimly remembering something, then he twigged. This must be the job Kev had told him about, the big job that was going to save the building firm that Mr White worked for and save his job. They were going to build houses on this land.

Pity. The great trees that screened Bryce's sports field from the overgrown green tangle were just on the turn. In a month they would be burning, all marvellous in their autumnal orange and gold. They were thick with untidy black nests and noisy birds flapped in and out of them endlessly. Some of the trees would surely have to go when the diggers moved in. Unless someone objected of course. That was the kind of thing weaselly Alex Brodey's parents went in for.

There he was, just getting off the bus with Kev. Most people were hurrying, the bus had been held up at the level crossing, but they didn't seem bothered, they were just dawdling along. 'Hey, Kev!' Baz shouted, pointing to the notice. 'Isn't Ridgeways your dad's firm? What's all this about then?' He knew, he just wanted a semi-human response from his best friend.

'New houses, thicko.'

'Well, that's great, that's really great, Kev. Good news for your dad, I mean.' No reply and Kev went off towards the gates of the Comprehensive.

'See you, Kev.' Baz yelled in desperation. 'Come round.' Then when there was still no response, he repeated, '*See you.*' If their friendship was over nobody could say that he'd not tried. Besides, he did miss Kev. He was the only person he could talk to about Dad, and he needed to, sometimes. Getting into this school had made the need stronger.

On the first day of term Bryce's started ten minutes later than on other days, so although all the neat grey-green figures were scurrying madly up the long drive, Baz didn't actually need to hurry. He was glad, because he couldn't. His insides suddenly felt like a load of fishermen's maggots, churning round endlessly in their riverside tin, and when he read the second notice behind the fence it was as if those bullies on the bus had kicked him in the stomach: 'Bryce's Academy', it said, 'founded 1532, Headmaster S. Lyme, MA (Oxon)'. Elegant gold letters against glossy dark green, to match the uniform, no doubt. This was *it*. Bryce's was a real place. He'd arrived, and he had to follow the others up that drive.

He never thought he'd be pleased to see Fat Alice, but when he saw her getting out of a taxi he nearly ran up and hugged her and he felt suddenly ashamed of himself for having given her the slip at home. She had a sticking-plaster on her knee and she hobbled up to him. It was odd, but fat girls, he noticed, were often very neat and tidy, their movements controlled, their voices low. It was as if they wanted to think slim, even if they weren't. Alice was certainly very neatly turned out this morning, but her round pink face was patchy and her eyes red. She'd definitely been crying. He said awkwardly, 'What's happened to you then?'

'You weren't there, when I came, Baz. Why didn't you wait? We'd agreed. Mummy phoned about it.'

'Thought we were going to be late,' he grunted, unconvincingly. 'Sorry, I was a bit nervous. I thought I ought to start off, it's such a long walk.'

'Well, wait tomorrow. I missed the bus because of you. It set off just as I got to the stop. There's a big crack in the pavement and I've hurt my knee. Daddy's going to write to the Council.'

They'd started to crunch up the long gravelled drive, Baz tense and silent, Alice prattling beside him. He was wrong about fat girls trying to merge into the scenery. Her voice was loud and penetrating, just like her mother's. As they walked she was actually trying to tuck her arm into his, as if they were a pair of old-age pensioners. 'Don't,' he muttered, shaking her off.

'Oh, sorry,' and she disengaged herself good-naturedly. That was one thing about Alice Sugden, you couldn't offend her very easily.

'Why did you stop piano lessons with Mummy?' she inquired. 'She said you were doing really well.'

Suddenly he was embarrassed. Why did she have to ask *that*, now, when the great pile of Bryce's school loomed up before them with its wedding-cake turrets and its rows of gleaming windows, its flag flying, its great sweeps of neatly clipped grass, its vast Rugby pitches. He could hardly look at the place. He wanted to run home, back to Inkerman Street. With a swift well-practised movement he raised his hand to his right ear, slipped out the gold ring and buried it in the fluff inside his trouser pocket.

'Oh,' he said vaguely, 'it all got a bit expensive for my mum.' He looked down at his green uniform. 'This lot cost a bomb too, and most of it's second-hand.'

She picked a hair off the collar of his blazer and snuggled up. 'You always look smart Baz. No one would know.'

'*Get off*, Alice, for Heaven's sake . . .'

'Oh, sorry,' but nothing could crush her for more than half a minute. 'Mummy told me you'd got the best mark in the scholarships,' she went on in her bright penetrating voice. 'She says you are Number One.'

'Am I? Honestly?'

'Yes. She found out at the open evening, at the end of the summer term.'

'Oh. Well Mum couldn't get to that, she had to work and I didn't like going on my own.'

'You could have come with us, Baz, you can come with us to things any time.'

'Thanks.' But he had no intention of accompanying the Sugdens to anything. Mummy, Daddy and Alice were fat, short and squat, resembling a family of toby jugs. Funny that his mother hadn't told him that he was Bryce's Number One scholar. Was it because of those little hints she dropped now and again that he could be a bit big-headed, a bit full of himself? *Number One!* Baz felt inches taller as they reached the top of the drive and stared at the dozens of grey-green figures as they milled about in a vast playground to the right of the famous clock tower. *Number One*. He was as good as anyone else here. So was Alice, he told himself loyally. She was being really great to him today. He vowed then and there to try to be a bit more patient with her. She could be so irritating though.

'Where do you suppose the new people go?' he said. Nobody else in the playground had their lost, new look. They all seemed very well established, chatting easily in little groups or playing games. Someone was listening to a portable radio. That was hopeful, anyhow. Baz wouldn't have thought they allowed those, at Bryce's.

They didn't. From a door under the clock tower two figures emerged in black gowns. One was short, dapper, and as bald as an egg, with oversized ears, the other loomed over him, his bristling eyebrows, and beaked nose gave him the look of a gigantic rook as his gown flapped round his legs. They paused momentarily under the clock, the little man jerking his head to left and to right as he inspected the playground, rubbing his hands. The curved beak of the taller one sniffed the air, obviously scenting trouble, and a voice suddenly rang out across the asphalt. 'Boy! Switch that off immediately and report to Mr Moncrieff, First Break!'

Across the crowded playground an instant silence fell as the offender pressed his Off button. Baz shivered as the two teachers swept past them down the drive, partly through nerves, but partly through admiration. Nobody at the Comprehensive *ever* got an instant response like that, not even Mr Greaves.

'He's called Slime,' Alice whispered. 'S. Lyme, that's what it says on the notice. Did you see his *nose*?' and she tittered.

'Couldn't really miss it, could you?' and Baz tittered back. 'What about the little one's *ears* though . . .' and they giggled again.

Then a bell rang, loud and imperious from somewhere up in the clock tower, at which all the greenies started to cluster together more thickly, moving vaguely towards various doorways.

This seemed to panic Alice. 'Come on,' she said, grabbing Baz's arm.

'Get off, can't you.'

'Well, come *on*. I'm going to ask somebody. That boy looks about our age, he might be in our class.'

'No, don't ask him, Alice.' It was the black boy from the bus queue, the one with the expensive leather satchel, the one

22

who had sneered about Inkerman Street. But it was too late. Alice's voice pierced the quiet of the emptying playground, turning the remaining heads in their direction.

'Er, excuse me, can you tell me where the new people are supposed to go?'

The boy stopped in his tracks and stared at her. The look was distinctly unfriendly. Alice might have been something that had crawled out from underneath a stone.

'We're in 3M,' she explained brightly. 'I'm Alice Sugden, and this is Baz Bradshaw.'

'I know. We've met. I'm in 3M too as it happens. It's Mr Moncrieff's class. You need B corridor, it's the room at the far end,' and he turned away and walked off.

'Charming,' muttered Baz, as they followed him inside. But Alice didn't seem to have noticed. She was now prattling on about her trumpet lessons. 'Did I tell you about this jazz group I'm in?' she chirped brightly. 'It's called Ultimate Sound. I used to have lessons with Mr Goodearl at the Tech, but I'm having them here, from now on. Mummy says their brass teacher is second to none. I suppose that's what we're paying for, the best teachers. Are you starting an instrument, Baz?'

'Nope, and anyhow we're not *paying*. We're the scholarship kids, and people will say things about that, just you wait.'

'What kind of things?' Alice was all wide-eyed innocence.

'Just things,' he croaked. Baz's voice had somehow dried up. He was feeling sick with nerves.

Alice glanced at him. 'It'll be fine,' she said with a hennish cluck of reassurance. 'You're Number One remember, and you can start an instrument any time. Listen, you can always have a go on my trumpet.'

'Thanks a million.'

Kev and Alex hadn't yet reached school, in fact, they'd got no further than some bushes on Pullen's Field where they were having a quiet smoke. Kev said he couldn't face school without a cigarette first. Alex said he wasn't sure he could face school

23

at all, but he might go down town instead. It was Alex who had started Kev smoking, in the summer holidays. It made him feel slightly sick. He did it to keep Alex company he supposed, and because he had this unpleasant way of calling you 'chicken' if you disagreed with him about anything. It was funny, though, Alex smoking. His parents were paranoid about cigarettes, they belonged to ASH, the anti-smoking society, and there was a big *No Smoking* notice in their hall. That was why Alex had started. The more his parents went on about things to him the worse he was. His latest thing was aerosol sprays. He had just done a demonstration for Kev, on a tree. 'Save this tree,' it now said, in thick white blobby letters. 'My mother'll be round at Ridgeways,' he said, 'just as soon as she knows about this housing scheme. She makes us use recycled bog-paper at home. She's saving the rain forests.'

'Sounds disgusting.'

'*It is*. Do you know, if you —'

'Shh!' Kev hissed. 'Somebody's coming. Get down!' Feet were crunching down towards them over the crisp autumn leaves and they could hear voices earnestly discussing the future of Pullen's Field. The two boys ducked neatly into the bushes, stamping their cigarettes out.

'This must go, Barraclough,' Slime was saying to a gentle-faced elderly man in brown overalls, Ted Barraclough, caretaker at Bryce's school for thirty-five years. 'You can just lay it flat in the grass and they can come and pick it up.'

'But it will rot, sir. The leaves won't do it any good.'

'Well, let it rot. Ridgeways have no right to put it up. They've jumped the gun, so serve them right. What do you say, Henry?'

'Oh, absolutely, sir, they have no right, no right at all,' and Mr Moncrieff rubbed his hands together enthusiastically as the caretaker scratched his head and inspected Ridgeway's notice.

'As it happens, Henry, I've had confirmation of our deal this morning *and* an outline plan of the new courts from Hender-

24

son's. Sir Albert has been on the phone too, needless to say. Do you know, we are going to end up with the best sports facilities in the North-West? Not bad, eh, for a school of our size?'

'Really, sir? Well, that's marvellous.'

'Yes, I think so,' Slime said complacently. 'What with the extra tennis-courts and our brand-new computer block the next school prospectus is going to look pretty good, don't you know?'

'Mmm. It's a pity some of these trees will have to go.'

'Well, not *all* of them, Henry, and the whole thing is going to look a lot more attractive than those poky little houses that Ridgeways were going to build.'

'Quite, headmaster. Now, about the new people. Good heavens, I've just seen the time, we must get back. If I could just have a word . . .'

'Carry on Mr Barraclough,' Slime called magisterially over his shoulder as the two men crunched up the drive towards the school buildings. Alex and Kev, who had heard every word, emerged cautiously from the bushes as Mr Barraclough stumped after the disappearing black figures muttering something about fetching a spade.

'That was *disgusting*,' Kev said, lighting a second cigarette and snorting angrily. 'Dad said there was a problem about this building project. He's been whinging on about it for ages, saying he might get his cards if it didn't go through.'

'Well, it's not going through, is it? The school has obviously bought it, to make tennis-courts.'

'That disgusts me too. Ever seen their courts? It's like Wimbledon at Bryce's.'

They sat and smoked in angry silence. Then through the trees came the faint but persistent dinning of an electric bell from the Comprehensive. Kev checked his watch and shot to his feet. 'Heck, Alex, it's 9 o'clock, come *on*.'

'In a minute, in a minute. Look at this,' and he hopped over the fence and back into the road.

25

The new aerosol was brilliant and Alex had a very steady hand, in fact he was quite artistic. There was nobody on Stockport New Road. The kids were all in school and the shoppers weren't out yet. It took only seconds for him to decorate the fence in gigantic white letters. The message was 'BRYCE'S STINKS.'

4

Alice and Baz lost the boy with the satchel the minute they got inside the school buildings. 'He might have waited,' Alice said reproachfully, as they stood huddled nervously together, like novice swimmers indecisive on the edge of a pool, as great streams of neatly-uniformed children surged this way and that along shiny echoing corridors.

'Ne'er. Not that one,' grunted Baz. 'He ignored me in the bus queue. I tried to get him talking but he wasn't interested. He's pretty snobby I'd say.'

'Just shy, probably,' Alice said charitably. 'Look, there's a plan of the school over there. That'll tell us where places are.'

They crossed the corridor and examined it. Next to the plan was a big stone plaque decorated with flags, lions and trumpets, listing the names of boys from Bryce's who had died in two world wars. It made Baz think of his father. The day after the thing had happened strangers had put wreaths of flowers on the pavement outside the building society. Mum cried when she heard.

'Fantastic,' Alice said in a whisper, 'all those people giving their lives for their country, all from this school.'

'It wasn't only Bryce's,' Baz said stoutly. 'I bet there were just as many from our school as well.' But it wasn't 'his' school any more. The untidy, friendly Comp felt a million miles away from this vast echoey place with its gowns and its solemn carved memorials. At this moment he wanted it back. He felt he was being disloyal to it, accepting the scholarship, and he couldn't forget how Kev had treated him ever since the letters had arrived. That was painful, after they'd been such mates.

When they found the class-room they hovered outside the

open door. About twenty children were already inside, installing themselves and their belongings amongst the rows of battered old-fashioned desks with white china ink-wells. Baz felt against his inside pocket to check he'd got his new fountain-pen. There were rules here, of course, about exactly what you were allowed to write with: no Biros, no felt-tips and no bottles of ink to be brought to school in case of accidents. Honestly, *Bryce's Rules*. They went on and on and *on*, marvellous for getting you off to sleep at night. Miles better than counting sheep.

The boy with the satchel who'd given them the slip was already standing in the middle of a small group, holding forth very volubly. 'The boy's brilliant,' they heard, 'according to my uncle, anyhow, this year's top scholar. Huh, looks a bit ape-like if you ask me. Now the fat girl's something else, fifteen stone I'd say and she's down for trumpet lessons on the music rota. I think it must be dangerous for someone of her size. She'll bust a gut if she's not careful.'

Nervous, rather uncertain, laughter rippled amongst the desks as Baz, screwing up all his courage, pushed Alice in front of him and entered the form-room. 'Can we sit anywhere?' he said in a loud defiant voice to the first person he met, a gangling clever-faced boy with heavy black spectacles and dark floppy hair. He felt ready to kill the other one, the boy with the satchel, and so sorry for Alice, who'd flushed beetroot-red at the 'fat girl' remarks and whose little button mouth was definitely trembling.

'Sure,' the boy said, 'here, these two desks are free. I'll just move my stuff off. Jugsy will put us all where he wants us anyhow, he won't have the baddies at the back for example, so it doesn't really matter.'

'Are you a baddie then?' inquired Baz.

'Sure I am,' and the boy grinned. 'All the best people are, in this place.'

Alice sat down, propped her shiny new school case in front of her, and retreated behind it. Baz dumped his banana bag on the adjoining desk and stared round the class-room focusing finally on the boy who'd been sneering about them, daring him to go on. But there was now complete silence in the class-room; all eyes were glued upon him and Alice.

The boy who'd made space for them grinned across, sympathetically, Baz felt, and flicked a long black lock of limp straight hair out of his eyes.

'I'm Alice Sugden,' Alice said, half whispering because of the sudden awful quiet, 'and my friend's Basil Bradshaw. We both live on Inkerman Street.'

Baz could have killed her, because it was quite obvious that the boy with the satchel hadn't finished with them. He was listening hard. 'Near the slipper factory, folks,' he announced to the whole room. 'Best end of town,' and he sniggered.

'My gran lives on Inkerman Street,' the dark-haired boy told Alice, 'Mrs Pollitt. She lives at number Thirty Six. I'm Ed Pollitt, but call me Polly. Everyone else does.'

'I'm Baz,' Baz said solidly and loudly. 'Baz Bradshaw. No one calls me Basil.'

Polly stared at him with interest. 'Baz Bradshaw,' he muttered, then repeated the name, 'Baz *Bradshaw*. Hey, I know that name, are you famous or something?'

'Not that I've heard,' Baz said, diving into his banana bag. He didn't need anything from it, he just didn't want any more questions. Alice, instantly responding to Polly's friendliness, had sidled up to him. Baz stared at her disapprovingly. She always had to get so *close* to people. Why didn't someone tell her about it?

'He's this year's top scholar,' she said proudly.

'*Alice* –' he warned, 'leave it can't you?'

'Oh, I know,' Polly said warmly, 'Simon's just been telling us. Mega-brilliant, obviously.' But Polly really didn't *sound* sarcastic, and it looked like genuine admiration in his startled-looking blue eyes, spaced widely apart and separated by a comical turned-up snub nose. He said, 'I'm sure I read a thing in the paper about someone called Bradshaw . . .'

'It'd be about his dad, Polly,' Alice explained, reverential now and giving Baz one of her hen-like, protective smiles.

'Shut up,' he said, 'about my dad. We *agreed*.'

'But Baz, Polly only —'

'I *said* shut up.'

Polly instantly got the message, that the subject of Baz's father was not for human consumption. 'OK, Baz,' he said expansively, 'if you're not famous, are you Green?'

'You what?' Baz had emerged from the depths of his banana bag and was staring hard at Polly, wondering whether, in this harsh-seeming Bryce's world, he could be trusted, whether he was friend or foe. So far they'd only met foes.

'Green. You've got to have heard about the Greens, Baz. I hope your mum's shopping is all biodegradable for a start. And does she send you to the bottle-bank with all her glass-ware? You do *use* glass containers at your house, don't you, because plastic is a scourge, it's practically indestructible. The oceans of the world are awash with plastic squeegy bottles. Did you know that?'

'No, no, I didn't,' Baz muttered. What was this boy on about? 'I've never thought about it,' he added, 'to be honest.'

'OK, friend, well now's the time to *get* thinking. Here, have one of these.' On Polly's desk was a small pile of green leaflets. He peeled a couple off and presented them to Alice and Baz. 'How to be friendly to the Earth,' they read. 'Join your local Green Party.'

Baz was suspicious. Was this boy Polly just being friendly to get something out of them? 'How much is it to join?' he said.

'Nothing, to people in school. They want our support, that's all. Now I suggest —'

'Psst! Jugsy . . . Jugsy.' Someone on guard at the class-room door must have spotted movement at the end of the corridor. Polly whipped his leaflets smartly into his desk and sat down.

'Why is he called Jugsy?' Alice queried, as a shadow crossed the threshold. All bags were now removed from desk lids and all hands composed tidily in front of neat green blazers.

'It's the ears. Go for the ears,' Polly whispered back with a grin. 'Actually he's called Moncrieff. Oh, and, by the way, he's brain dead, just in case you don't notice.'

Alice didn't dare laugh, nobody did. 'Jugsy' had arrived and was now standing quite rigid in front of the teacher's desk, staring at them all. The atmosphere in the class-room had turned to ice. Not a muscle moved among the silent, apprehensive rows, not a hair, not an eyelid. Even the stray fly, left over from summer, that had been bumbling hopelessly against a window pane in hope of release to the great outdoors, suddenly gave up the ghost and plopped out of sight and into silence. It was as if the Snow Queen of the fairy story had entered the class-room of 3M on B corridor.

There, however, any resemblance ended. 'Jugsy' was the little bald man whom they'd seen crossing the playground with Slime, the headmaster.

Alice and Baz were uncomfortably close to him, on the front row. They watched as he inspected his table and chair minutely, for dust presumably, though like everything else at Bryce's they looked and smelt recently polished. Alice marvelled at the multiple folds of his black gown, each minute pleat immaculate, not a crease in sight. Every week her mother ironed surplices for the church choir and pleats like that were killers, she was always complaining about them. Baz was concentrating on the teacher's head. It was marvellously bald and highly polished, to match the furniture. The enormous jug-handle ears were exactly symmetrical, clamped on to his head. It looked as if you could take hold of them, pull up sharply and so separate head from neck. It was cruel, what some people had to put up with.

But the minute Jugsy opened his mouth any lingering shreds of pity vanished in a puff of smoke. He had a thin, steely voice and he barked out his words staccato, as if he was spitting out metal staples. 'Sit,' he commanded, in response to a polite, 'Good morning, Mr Moncrieff,' from the class. No 'please', no 'nice to see you all back after the holidays'. Just 'sit'. Baz settled gloomily into his place. He'd got bad vibes.

'We have two additions to 3M this term,' spat Jugsy, glancing at Alice and Baz but with no welcoming smile. As he talked he constantly rubbed together his extremely pink, small hands. He couldn't seem to *stop* doing it. Guilt that was, the constant rubbing of hands. Baz had read it somewhere. Jugsy could be some kind of sadist, the kind that beats boys to death. Did they have canes at Bryce's? It wouldn't really surprise him.

'Alice Sugden and Basil Bradshaw,' he said. 'If you read your local newspaper, and I sincerely hope you do, you will know that Alice and Basil have won scholarships to Bryce's. Well done, both children,' and he clapped limply. The class followed suit, all equally limp. Baz felt as if they'd come last in a three-legged race.

'I'm not a man to waste time,' Jugsy went on crisply, 'Scholarships are all very well, but the theme here is work . . . *Work*. Now then, Registration, which proceeds by numbering off. Bradshaw you are, er . . . number 1.'

'*Told* you,' whispered Alice, beaming across the row and prodding him.

'Silence!' spat Jugsy. 'When I want your opinion, Sugden, I'll ask for it. The number allotted to Bradshaw is merely alphabetical. You are number . . . 17. Very well, begin, Bradshaw.'

In silence the class called out their numbers and for the third time since leaving home Baz felt he wanted to murder someone. First there'd been that bullying in the bus queue, then the black boy with the satchel getting at them again, just before Jugsy appeared, now this, Alice made to feel a total ninny, because of a harmless mistake. And he hated the way Jugsy called everyone by their second name, girls as well as boys. Mum had told him they might do that here, that it was the thing to do in schools like Bryce's. He thought it was hateful.

He stared round as people shouted their numbers out. 3M looked a boring lot, with very few exceptions. Polly seemed

OK, at least he'd shown them some human kindness, and there was an interesting-looking bloke at the back too, a boy called James Elder. Baz knew his name because Jugsy had already told him off twice for talking and also warned him about getting his hair cut. It was fantastic, an unruly orange mop. He had a clown's face, big lips, chubby pink cheeks, pointy ears and all under the marvellous ginger mop. He couldn't keep still either, he kept jigging about and dropping things. Baz predicted that Jugsy would pick on him, when anything went wrong. There was always someone like that in a class.

The prettiest girl was called Vanessa Honeywell. She was having lessons on the French horn. That was even more difficult than the trumpet, wasn't it? It was hard to imagine her all red in the face and puffing, she was so small and slight with a perfect ivory skin and long dark hair done up in a single plait. It didn't look old-fashioned on her, nothing would, she was too beautiful. Alice saw him looking at her when she explained about her horn lessons, and she pouted jealously. He was going to have trouble with Alice; if only she didn't live just up the street. She behaved as if she owned him or something.

People sniggered when she said she played the trumpet, but Jugsy immediately froze them into embarrassed silence. That was good, anyhow. Grudgingly, Baz awarded him a couple of Brownie points for that. Then he wrote some Latin on the blackboard, 'Deus Dat Incrementum'. 'Can anyone translate our school motto?' he said, warming up a few degrees and with the faint suggestion of a smile. 'I feel the new people should know it. Anyone like to tell them?'

Baz's hand shot up. 'Please, sir, I will, Oh *please*, sir . . .'

But he'd made a tactical mistake, being enthusiastic. He could hear people muttering 'Big-head' and 'Show-off'.

'You *know*, Bradshaw? Did you do Latin at your Comprehensive?'

'No, sir, but it was in that book we got sent, when I won

'. . . that book, you know.' He knew he mustn't talk about the scholarship at all, he could feel waves of hostility.

'Oh, I do know, Bradshaw. Can anyone else translate?'

'God gives us our pay rises, sir,' muttered Orange Mophead, doodling on a pad. There was a general ripple of nervous laughter, but Jugsy was clearly not amused. 'Bradshaw,' he said, 'kindly translate.'

'God gives us the increase, sir.'

'Correct. Elder, an essay please on my desk tomorrow morning. Four sides, A4. Title: *Insolence*. Thank you very much.'

Appalled, Baz and Alice exchanged looks.

'He's a pig,' someone whispered. But fortunately Jugsy didn't seem to hear. Mophead went on doodling busily.

'Is that *clear* Elder?'

'OK, sir.'

'And don't say *OK*!'

As he spoke Jugsy opened a drawer and placed a thick block of A4 paper on his desk, as if in anticipation of further trouble and more essays. Then he buried his neat pink thumbs in his gown and rocked back on his heels. 'Before you fill in your timetables, er – give these forms out please, Pollitt – I've got some exciting news for you.' He made this announcement with all the passion of a squashed worm. Did *anything* excite him? Latin perhaps? Baz would soon know, he took the beginners set. He and Alice were in it. Oh heck.

'Sir Albert Anderson, our famous old boy, has made a further generous gift to the school so that we can now buy the land adjoining rugger pitch B and convert it into extra tennis-courts. This purchase will save the land from becoming a housing development and, of course, will bring immense benefit to the school.'

Polly, half-way round the class delivering timetable forms, with which he had sneakily included his 'Friendly to the Earth' leaflets, one to every desk, stopped in his tracks and stared back at Jugsy. 'Sir?'

'Yes, Pollitt – come on, come on, get these timetables out, please, we've not got all day.'

'Well, sir, that waste ground is Pullen's Field.'

'I am well aware of that, Pollitt, and thanks to a silly legal dispute it's been sadly neglected, and underused for far too long. Now thanks to Sir Albert's generosity –'

'But, sir –'

'You have interrupted me, Pollitt, and we really must get on . . .'

'But, sir,' Polly went on heatedly, clearly not caring whether he'd interrupted or not, 'tennis-courts will be no better than houses. Some of the trees'll go, and the wildlife. It'll all be destroyed.'

Jugsy's mouth flopped open and shut rhythmically. He resembled an outsized goldfish on its way to a funeral. Baz saw that, for the first time, he was definitely off his guard. There were mutterings and rustlings round the class about Polly 'boring on' about the Green issue and 'how Green you are'. Taking a deep breath, Baz put up his hand. Jugsy looked distinctly wary. 'Yes, Bradshaw? What have you go to say for yourself?'

'Them houses, sir –'

'Those houses young man, *those*.'

Someone sniggered, whispering something about 'grammar' and why couldn't he get a haircut, along with James Elder. It was that boy with the posh satchel, Simon Speirs. But Baz didn't care, it was Kev he was thinking about now. He said urgently, 'My friend's dad will be out of a job if they don't build those houses, sir, and any road –'

'I beg your pardon, Bradshaw?'

'Any . . . anyway – we've got tennis-courts, haven't we, sir, and it's not like houses. I mean people need them to live in.'

Jugsy folded his arms and assumed a bland, flat smile. 'Bradshaw, do look to your grammar please, when the glory of your own rhetoric carries you away. As I say, thanks to the great generosity of Sir Albert we will soon have another six much-needed tennis-courts, and next summer, when you are all busy lobbing and volleying, I've no doubt you will all be grateful to him. Now, another excitement: your timetables.'

Polly, now back in his place, put his hand up again. 'Yes, Pollitt?' there was no disguising Jugsy's impatience now.

'Is that the end of the discussion, sir?'

'It is Pollitt. We can't take up any more valuable time and I —' But he suddenly dried up. A green paper pellet from somewhere at the back, expertly aimed and angled, had hit him smartly on the chin. 'Who threw *that*?' There was absolutely no reaction. But, as Jugsy uncrumpled the ball of paper and read about being friendly to the earth and recycling your bottles and using recycled toilet-paper, the whole class, involuntarily, took in its breath sharply. 'Who is responsible for this?' and Jugsy held up the bedraggled leaflet by a finger and thumb, as if it were something diseased.

'Edward Pollitt gave them out with the timetables, sir.' It was Simon Speirs, Baz had already labelled him Creep Number One, now he awarded him the Creeps Medal with Bar.

'I see. Is this *true*, Pollitt?'

'Yes, sir, but it's a good cause, sir, and honestly I was only —'

'Silence. On my desk tomorrow morning, four sides of A4, in ink. Title: *Disobedience, compounded by ... Subversive Behaviour*. Thank you.'

'But, sir —'

'Would you like me to make it eight sides, Pollitt?'

'No, sir.'

'Very well. Now then, if I don't know within five minutes the identity of the phantom pellet thrower, the whole form will stay in after school for two hours.'

Mophead got to his feet. 'I threw it, sir.'

'You did? May I ask why?'

'Dunno, sir. Suppose I was bored.'

'Right, well we can always find a cure for boredom, here you are, four more sheets of A4. Come on, come on, take them. I've not got all day. In ink for tomorrow morning . . . Title: *The mindless majority*. You have a busy evening ahead, Elder, especially as you need to fit a haircut in too. Bradshaw, the need for a good haircut applies to you also. I shall inspect both heads tomorrow morning.'

The next few minutes were taken up by Jugsy chalking a complicated timetable of lessons, sets and homework assignments on to the blackboard. Then the class bent over their desks and began to copy everything out.

'Wonder what they're doing next door?' Baz whispered to Alice when Jugsy was safely at the back, sorting out a clash of lessons for Mophead.

'Did you say something, Bradshaw?'

(He'd forgotten just how large those jug handles were.)

'No, sir.' Well he'd not, nothing relevant or important, anyway.

'Oh, forgive me. I rather thought you did.'

This end of Bryce's property was quite close to that of the Comprehensive, the waste ground of Pullen's Field, which separated the two schools being roughly triangular and tapering almost to nothing at the top of the slope. You couldn't actually see anything of the Comp, as there was a row of great gloomy conifers in the way. But you could hear things. As he sat there, Baz could hear the familiar tinny whirring of an electric bell and the first voices, juniors, let out for Early Break. He felt sad, almost deprived. What had he given up and what was he *doing* here? It was like some concentration camp left over after the war.

5

At break in the playground, Simon Speirs had a go at him. People were standing about in little knots, chattering, and it was funny, each group had a certain *look* about it. 'Jake' Elder (it was Jake to his friends he'd told Baz, so *that* was quite promising) was in the middle of a wild-looking bunch that was horsing about with a football and making too much noise, according to the duty master, who prowled wolfishly up and down the vast asphalted yard along invisible straight lines, back and forth. One of them was listening to a Walkman, which was confiscated by the master the minute he saw it. Baz was interested; he'd like to have asked why. At his old school you could listen to your Walkman at break and dinner, so long as you didn't disturb other people. They were brilliant inventions, he thought, particularly when you wanted to be on your own and didn't feel like talking. When he'd got more established here he might ask someone just why they were banned. Rules should have some logic behind them and there were too many rules at Bryce's.

Simon Speirs was in a group he'd already labelled 'Squeaky Clean'. They were on the other side of the yard from Jake and the Wild Bunch, talking rather formally in a tight little circle, mainly boys, all excessively neat with their immaculate hair-cuts, polished shoes and brilliant crisp, white shirts. Baz felt slightly nervous about his soft blue one. Mum had bought two of them from the Matron, so they had to be 'correct', hadn't they? But why were all the others in white?

He stood against a wall where nobody could get at him, flanked by the faithful Alice and by Vanessa Honeywell, who had just been showing her where the girls' cloakroom was.

Vanessa. She didn't have much to say for herself but she really was a good-looker. She ought to play something like a cello he decided, running his eyes admiringly over the glossy pigtail, or a flute. French horns made rude noises and he couldn't associate that sort of thing with a girl like her. 'Are you going to like it, Baz?' Alice said chirpily. 'Vanessa says it's a great school.'

'Dunno, yet. Everything seems so *strict*. I mean, why are Walkmans banned, for Heaven's sake?'

'Oh, Slime thinks things like that distract us from our work,' Vanessa told him. 'Anyhow, people steal them. There was so much hassle about Walkmans last term, he just said that was it, that nobody could have them anymore.'

'Jugsy's a maniac,' Baz said. 'All those essays he dished out this morning. What's eating him?'

'Well, it's that kind of school, Baz,' explained Alice solemnly.

'*What* kind of school?'

'Everything's taken very seriously.'

'Huh, don't see what's wrong with a bit of a joke. And why do they have to use our surnames? It's horrible, that, it's like having a number.'

'Yes,' Vanessa said sympathetically, 'I hate it too. But my dad says it's what they've always done at the great big public schools, it's supposed to give us, you know . . .'

'Class?' Baz said suspiciously.

'That sort of thing.'

He stared across the yard at the Squeaky Clean group. They were slowly breaking up and one or two of them, including Simon Speirs and the senior boy called Julius, who'd bullied the little ones in the bus queue, were making their way towards him, purposefully he felt, his heart doing a sudden, unexpected little flip.

'That's the wrong kind of shirt, friend,' Simon said as he came up. Crooking his finger under the knot of Baz's tie, he flipped it out and then poked him in the chest.

'What do you mean?' Baz stepped out from the cover of the wall, stood his ground and restored the tie to the V of his green sweater. It had suddenly gone very quiet and he could hear heavy breathing from Alice. For once he was grateful for her reassuring pink bulk.

'It shouldn't have buttons on the collar, and anyhow, it's the wrong colour, it's supposed to be white. They've changed the clothing regulations.'

'It can't be wrong, my mum got it at the school sale.'

'Oh, it's all right folks, his *mum* got it, at the school sale,' and some of the Squeaky Clean people laughed. This was Julius, doing a brilliant imitation of Baz's Lancashire accent. He didn't have a local accent himself and neither did Simon Speirs. They both spoke like news-readers on the telly.

'The school doesn't sell shirts,' Simon informed him.

'Yes it does, this shirt came from the matron. She ran a second-hand sale, back in the summer.' The minute it was out Baz wished he could bite it back. You couldn't tell that any item of his Bryce's uniform was second-hand, Mum had done such a marvellous job with everything. But the point was, she didn't earn all that much money so she couldn't have bought all new, like Alice's mother. Anyhow, lots of parents had gone to that sale. Not everyone at Bryce's was stinking rich.

Simon Speirs burst into loud, forced laughter. 'Oh, you got it from *The Cow* did you? Trust her to sell you a dud shirt,' and he started to finger the collar buttons.

'*Leave off!*' Baz said dangerously, shaking himself free. He didn't like this. They were all looking at him curiously, as if he was some kind of interesting pet, and they were getting too close, somehow edging up when you didn't notice.

'Don't see what's wrong with having a button-down collar, do you Alice? Do you, Vanessa?' Neither spoke, they merely smiled sympathetically. They were obviously nervous too.

Then Julius had a go at him. 'The point is, Basil —'

'It's Baz, actually.'

'The point is, *Baz*,' (and he spat out the name as if it had four

40

letters, not three) 'that the shirt's not regulation. As a matter of fact, I could report you for having the wrong shoes, too,' and he fingered a blue and silver badge on his tie. It said 'Vice-prefect'.

'Could you really? Go in for Vice, do you?' Baz countered angrily.

'No.' But Julius didn't like the sarcasm. He'd flushed a deep furious red.

'Well, I think you do. I saw you bullying those little lads in the bus queue. I could report you to Slime for *that*, couldn't I? Two can play at your game.'

'Let's get back to your shoes, Bradshaw.'

'OK, let's, Malin.' He knew that was the boy's surname, from the prefect list in the main corridor.

'They've got patterns on them, and that's not allowed. It says plain black shoes. Can't your mother read?'

Instinctively Baz bunched his fists and stepped forward. 'Shut your mouth, about my mother. Do you want a fight, Malin? Is that what you came over here for, to fight? Because I'm good at fighting. We learn it, you know, in the jungle. We swing our banana bags at the natives. Or don't Vice-prefects go in for fights?'

Malin took a step towards him, half raising an arm, and the people listening held their breath. Then he turned away, muttering, 'Oh, drop dead,' and the whole Squeaky Clean group started drifting away too, sullen, deprived unexpectedly of its kill.

By the wall Baz collected himself, determined to remain cool, paying no attention to his wildly thumping heart. 'Who's he, when he's at home?' he asked Vanessa, pulling his collar straight and rearranging his tie, 'He's disgusting.'

'Oh, Julius Malin's one of the head's faves, he's very clever and he knows how to keep well in with the staff.'

'The smoothy type,' murmured Alice.

'Oh, yes, mega-smooth. I don't think he'd get away with his bullying if he didn't do so well in class, but he's brilliant, and somehow he never gets caught.'

41

'That's disgusting as well. Any road, I don't think I approve of prefects. *Vice*, huh! And why does he hang round with third years anyway?' That suggested to Baz that he hadn't got too much confidence, with his own age group.

Alice, solidly determined to be happy at Bryce's, with her hard-won scholarship, was all for smoothing things over. 'Take no notice, Baz,' she clucked. 'They were only like that because we're new. Your label's showing, by the way,' and she fiddled with the collar of his blazer.

'Oh, leave me *alone*, Alice. Listen, this school ... it's ridiculous. Who cares about two buttons on a shirt collar? And who cares about an ear-ring or two? It's mad this place, if you ask me.'

'Oh ear-rings are bad for you, Baz,' cautioned Alice. 'They can make your ears rot, apparently. Mummy says –'

'I don't want to *know* what Mummy says,' and Baz stormed off to stand in an empty bit of playground, feeling a fool because he didn't have anyone to talk to except tactless Alice.

Just inside a brick-arched entrance that led into the school buildings from the vast yard, Slime was pinning up a notice. Baz could see the hunched black figure inspecting his handiwork, neatening it up no doubt, making sure all the drawing-pins were of regulation size. Then he saw Jugsy bustle up and start talking to him. He moved rapidly out of their field of vision. Even at this distance one of them might spot non-regulation shirts and non-regulation shoes. Funny Jugsy hadn't said anything in class. He was beginning to feel an attack of persecution mania coming on.

'All calm on the Western Front, Henry?' Slime was saying genially, as Jugsy stopped by the notice-board.

'Oh, yes, headmaster, all serene. Prout's on duty.'

'Good. Well, there it is. My election announcement. If the country's going to have an election, I don't see why Bryce's should be left out, do you? I mean, *Prime Minister resigns*, all parties in *disarray* – it's stirring stuff, Henry. We live in interesting times.'

'Mmm.' The response from Jugsy, to say the least, was luke-warm.

'You don't sound too convinced?'

'Frankly I'm not. Old Chinese curse, headmaster, "May you live in interesting times". No, to be honest, I'm not too keen on this election idea. I've been with 3M all morning, and the main business of their lives seems to be trying to hit me with balls of paper, with silly chat, and downright general sloppiness. The Elder boy is getting worse, you know. That hair's grown at least a foot since summer and I –'

'Henry,' Slime cut in rather tetchily, 'what has this to do with my school election, or any election, come to that?'

'Well, my point is that the children won't be *interested*, headmaster. I mean I doubt if they even *know* about the Prime Minister resigning, and as for a General Election . . .'

'But it's early days, Henry. It'll warm up pretty quickly now, they'll hear their parents talking, and so on. That's the beauty of this,' and he tapped his immaculate notice. 'We're in at the *beginning*. I'm tired of schools like Bryce's being called fossils, Henry, nineteenth century, all that nonsense. I want to show people we move with the times, that our pupils know what's going on in the world. I can guarantee nobody will be running a school election next door,' and he cocked a superior thumb in the direction of the Comprehensive.

'No, and I think they're wise. I don't like the idea, head-master, I don't like it at all.'

'Oh, Henry, grow up,' Slime said rather wearily. 'It was all agreed at the staff meeting yesterday and the great majority were in favour. It's an excellent development, really excellent. We spoon-feed these children too much, Henry, and making them run their own election will get them thinking for themselves for once. Creativity, Henry, independence of mind. Think of the *school*.'

'I am thinking of it, headmaster, and I'm not convinced a thing like this won't lead to trouble. There'll be rowdyism, a general loss of control, and I do wish –'

But he stopped abruptly. Slime had put a warning hand on his arm. There was a boy standing under the archway. They didn't know it but he'd heard every word. There were no rules against minding your own business during break, rules about leaning against sun-warmed bricks, waiting for the bell to go. Baz had seen the boy hanging about near the notice-board five minutes ago. It was Julius Malin.

'Malin,' Slime said. 'I've got a little job for you. I'd like these notices distributing please, one for each form-room notice-board, and one each in the general areas in A, B and C corridors. Any spares you may keep. I'm sure you'll be interested. Run along.'

Julius glanced down at the bundle of papers and feigned innocence. 'School elections . . . great, sir . . . brilliant, yes I *am* interested . . . very. I'll do the corridors now, sir, I've got five minutes.'

'Good. Thank you, Malin. I'd be interested to see what you come up with, if you decide to run . . . No worries there, Henry,' he said complacently, as Julius disappeared.

'No, well, one wouldn't expect worries with Julius Malin, headmaster, bright boy, if a little high-spirited at times, good background, all that. No, it's the Elders of this world who worry me, and the Pollitts.'

'Oh, don't be such an old woman, Henry, it's only a bit of fun.'

'I wish I could agree, headmaster.'

The head walked away, and left Jugsy staring into the playground. Seeing the solitary figure of the new boy, Basil Bradshaw, his brow crumpled into a frown. There was just a chance that he too might prove difficult. It had been outrageous of him to argue about the tennis-court scheme for Pullen's Field. He'd only been at Bryce's five minutes.

It was a very long lunch-hour, and lunch itself had been good, bags of choice and lots of food. Baz was glad Mum wasn't having to pay. Lunches as good as that must cost money.

He'd noticed that teachers and prefects didn't have to queue. When they arrived they just went straight to the front. So the waiting got longer and longer for everyone else.

Mr Greaves at the Comprehensive hadn't allowed that. Unless the circumstances were really exceptional, everyone had waited their turn, even him, and he was the headmaster. Dad wouldn't have approved of queue-jumping. He'd been all for the rights of ordinary people. What would he have thought of Bryce's school? And what would he have thought of this idea of a school election? At least that wasn't just for the favoured few. Baz had read the notices. It wasn't only for the seniors, anyone could form a party and go in for it. Polly said they were having it because the Prime Minister had been forced to resign and there was going to be a General Election in the country. He was keen. He was going to stand for the Greens, in the school one.

Baz rather wished the bell would go. So far today there'd been no proper lessons at all, it had been all giving out books and paper, filling in endless lists and deciding on big projects which all had to be done by half-term. Everything was so deadly serious. It was the gowns that really got him. They reminded him of funerals, everyone draped in black. It upset him.

Anyhow, this afternoon he had a double games lesson – surely that'd got to be a bit more fun. Five minutes to go and he saw Julius Malin at it again, throwing his weight about. There was nobody on duty in the yard this time otherwise he surely wouldn't have risked it, not Julius, not one of Slime's golden boys. Not three yards away from Baz, holding court in the centre of his Squeaky Clean group, as before, he'd cornered a very small boy. Baz wasn't sure, but he thought it was the one whose cap had ended up in the puddle. 'I can't,' he was protesting, 'I can't, honestly, Julius. I've got a piano lesson. Mr Davies goes mad if you're late.' It *was* the same boy. Baz recognized the pathetic, high-pitched bird-like cheep. He edged a bit nearer. 'I said I want a can of Coke,' he heard. 'Oh, and while you're at it, fetch me some peanuts too. Here's the money. And bring me all the change. I know you. Now *move*. The tuck-shop will be closed in five minutes.'

'Aw, Jule,' the child protested, 'I've got Mr Davies. Can't you go yourself?'

'I *beg your pardon*?' The other boy's voice was hideous with sarcasm. 'Go *myself*? What do you think disgusting little wimps like you are *for* in this school. *Go myself*? Now move your feet, will you . . .'

'Ouch! Julius! Leave off, that hurts. OK I'm going, I'm going.' The small boy had just had his ear pulled hard by the spiteful Julius and he scuttled off, rubbing it, scattering coins across the asphalt as he dropped all the money, in his haste. 'And pick that up, creep,' Julius called after him. 'I know exactly how much I gave you,' and he laughed.

Baz suddenly waded in, grabbing him by the arm. He couldn't stand it any longer. 'Hey you, Malin. You got a thing about ears, or something? Why don't you leave little guys like that alone? He's right, why should he run errands for *you*? Why can't you go yourself?'

Julius stared at him coldly, totally confident in his well-groomed, impeccably-accented arrogance. 'I beg your pardon?' he repeated in mockery.

'I said why should he run errands for you?'

'He *should* because that's the way we do things here, the way we always have, new boy. His turn will come, don't worry. He'll be sending other little worms on his errands, one day. It's just a question of waiting.'

'Well if you ask me,' said Baz, 'it stinks.' Around them a little crowd was slowly gathering. Baz could see Alice frantically signalling him to get away from Malin, Polly looking a bit anxious, Jake Elder with the amazing hair staring at them silently, bemused and intrigued.

'But nobody's asking you are they, scholarship boy? Why don't you just go and eat a few bananas?' and he kicked at Baz's red bag which was lying at his feet. 'And while you're at it, get yourself a decent shirt,' and leaning forward he pulled at Baz's collar, ripping one of the buttons off.

There was a gasp from the expectant crowd, shock, tinged with hope. This was growing into an incident. They could smell trouble, and they rather wanted it.

They got it too. Baz, feeling at his neck and realizing what Julius had done, hesitated, squared him up, then lunged forward and punched him in the face. Julius staggered back, feeling at his cheek. 'You'll be sorry you did that, Bradshaw,' he hissed. 'You'll be extremely sorry,' and he went for him, diving at his legs, getting him on to the ground in seconds, and pinning both arms behind him in an iron-like grip, pummelling him hard in the chest. Baz couldn't speak because he couldn't breathe. Julius Malin wasn't a particularly heavy type, but he was six feet tall, several inches higher than the shorter, squarer, Baz, and he was bearing down on him with his whole weight. Someone had taught him how to fight like this. Perhaps he'd been to special classes.

Baz was frightened. He thought the boy would end up by cracking his ribs, if he didn't get off him. He spluttered, 'Get away from me. I can't breathe.' Malin leaned back on his heels, still on top of Baz. 'Take back what you said then.' He'd still got Baz's hands twisted behind his back, he was doing his pummelling and pounding one-handed, he was brilliant.

'I won't. This school stinks if it allows you to treat kids like that. And you're a louse, Malin.'

Julius gave a kind of roar, got him by the shoulders and made as if to bang his head against the ground. 'Julius,' someone shouted, 'leave off, that's bloody dangerous,' and somewhere in the crowd a girl screamed. Then Simon Speirs appeared from nowhere and tried to pull Julius to his feet, away from Baz. 'Jugsy's coming. It's Jugsy, for God's sake, Malin . . .'

But Julius hadn't quite finished. 'Louse yourself,' he spat out at Baz, getting up. 'Here, read this, it'll tell you all about this school election. If you think you can run this school better

47

than anyone else, here's your big chance, Clever-clogs.' Baz struggled and squirmed in an effort to work himself free, but now Julius was forcing his mouth open and pushing something between his lips, a screwed-up ball of paper. As he did so the clip of his steel watch-strap caught Baz's lower lip and cut it deeply. The blood was running down warm and salty when Jugsy appeared on the scene, looming over them both like a bat with little feet that wore polished brown brogues.

The white typed label on the brown door said 'Miss Jennifer Jersey, SRN'. Baz stared at it, raised a hand, then dropped it again. He could still taste the paper in his mouth and it was disgusting. He was supposed to knock on this door, but he felt too scared, after the telling-off Jugsy had given him. He'd never seen anyone so angry. It was odd though, he'd seemed personally upset by what had happened as well, kept going on about Bryce's and how scholarship winners brought added 'lustre' to the school and how Baz had spoiled all that. At one point he looked as though he was going to burst into tears, it was awful. There had been no talk of punishment for either of them. Malin had been sent to Dr Prout, the geography teacher, because he was his special tutor. At least he'd not got away scot-free, and he usually did, according to Vanessa Honeywell. They'd been talking in the lunch queue before the whole thing had happened. She'd actually invited him over to her house! Mum had warned him that, these days, the girls pursued the boys. Still, he wasn't complaining. There would *be* punishments, though, for both of them. It was that kind of place. Vanessa had warned him what might happen as he'd gone off to find the matron. Perhaps they'd both be expelled. He wasn't sure he'd mind so much.

That was silly. It had only been a playground scuffle that had got out of hand. He was going to do well at this place, he *must* do well, for Dad. He might even go in for this election, like Polly. Dad would approve. He'd been very interested in politics. But what sort of party could he *have*? He was pig-ignorant. It was no good consulting his mother. He loved her a lot but she wasn't really very bright and she never read the newspapers. His father had been the one.

Miss Jennifer Jersey, SRN. Behind the shiny brown door The Cow lay in wait. With a nickname like that she must be at least twenty stone with massive bosoms and coarse black hairs on her chin, like Alice's mum. *Ugh.* He'd told Jugsy his lip was OK but no, he'd insisted on 'Matron' looking at it, so here he was, missing his first session out on the hockey pitches with an overweight individual in a bright-purple track suit, a man called Mr Slack. Reluctantly he knocked on the door. 'Come in,' said a light young voice and he turned the handle rather more hopefully. He'd been half expecting a 'Moo'.

Jenny Jersey was indeed young, and extremely pretty. Not in the dark glossy style of Vanessa Honeywell, but in a blonde, fluffy sort of way. She was sitting in a small untidy room in an old armchair with all the stuffing coming out of it, and as Baz entered she removed her feet from a battered coffee-table where they'd obviously been comfortably propped as she sat and read a magazine. He thought he saw bright-red leg-warmers being whisked away out of sight as she stood up and smoothed down her green nurse's uniform. A small gas fire was hissing softly, rather lost in the middle of a high marble grate; in front of it, curled up in a gently snoozing ball, a large ginger cat was fast asleep.

'My goodness, lovey,' she said, when she saw his bleeding lip. 'What have you been up to? Here, sit down,' and she pointed to the saggy old chair. 'Want a cup of tea, I've just brewed up,' and she waved a mug at him.

'Thanks,' said Baz, and lowered himself into the armchair rather gingerly in case it collapsed. He was amazed at this snug oasis of normality buried at the end of C corridor in Bryce's school; and Matron wasn't cow-like at all, she was cool, with her scarlet leg-warmers and her tumbling hair, her tea-mugs that said 'I love Liverpool'.

'Sugar?'

'Yes please, one spoonful.'

'Here, you'd better have two. Sweetness is good for shock, matey,' she told him rather more severely, 'and I'd say you'd had one. You've been fighting, haven't you?'

'How did you guess?' His head was beginning to ache and his ribs hurt. Could Malin have cracked them?

'Now, now, no need to be sarky with me.' She was cleaning his lip up now with cotton wool and antiseptic. It stung.

'Sorry,' he muttered, into his Liverpool mug. She was nice and this room was nice. He didn't want to get on the wrong side of her.

'I heard there had been a fight, from one of the babies. Anyhow, your lip is bleeding. Who did you fight then, Superman?'

'Julius Malin. He was picking on one of the little lads.'

'So you socked him one?'

'Sort of. But he's bigger than me. Any road, he was brilliant. Really professional. You know.'

'Hmm ... if I know Julius Malin he'd be surprised to have someone sticking up for themselves. That was good. Not that I approve of fighting, Basil Bradshaw.'

He looked at her. 'How do you know my name?'

'Oh, The Cow keeps her ear to the ground. You won the top scholarship this time didn't you? I've heard quite a bit about you, Basil. And about your dad, of course.'

They exchanged a very long look. In the silence the gas fire bubbled and the ginger cat gave a contented little snore. *She knew.* But he couldn't talk about his father, not even to her. Get away from it Baz, quick, he told himself. Change the subject.

He said, 'Julius is brilliant at his work, too, isn't he?'

'Oh, yes. Maths is his big thing, I gather, and he's one of those computer geniuses. His father's firm has just fitted out the new computer block for us. Are you into computers, Basil?'

'No. We didn't have much chance to have a go on them at

our school. We had one, though,' he added loyally. Then he remembered, again, the Comp wasn't his place any more. It wasn't 'we' it was 'they'.

She said, with a frown, 'Julius is a bit of a lad on the quiet, but it's not like him to start a fight. He likes to keep on the right side of the law. What happened, exactly?'

'I told you, he was picking on this little lad who wouldn't go to the tuck-shop for him, and he twisted his ears, and I told him not to. Then he pulled a button off my shirt, said it wasn't regulation or something. Look, he's ripped it.'

He leaned forward and she examined the neck of his shirt. 'Oh heck, Basil, that was my fault. I sold that shirt to your mum at the summer sale. But they've changed the rules again. It's "white only" now. Mr Lyme's always jiggling with the uniform regulations. I reckon he just enjoys playing with his personal word processor, you know, "delete", "shift", "insert".'

'White only,' muttered Baz, not really listening, 'that's great,' and he stroked his coffee-coloured cheek.

The Cow ignored this. 'Don't be silly, Basil,' she said, with a sudden unexpected sharpness. 'This school's only interested in *brainpower*. It admits the best. It doesn't matter what colour you are or where you come from. Right? Now keep still and I'll sew that shirt up.'

Baz drank his tea while she found a sewing-box. Then she bent over him with needle and thread.

'Ouch!'

'Well *keep still*, can't you.'

'Do you want to know what I think?'

'Go on, what do you think?'

'That it's daft, all this heavy stuff about uniform. And another thing, in the bus Malin said I ought to take my ear-ring out.'

'Ear-rings? I don't blame him. The head would have had your guts for garters if you'd turned up in ear-rings. You should be grateful to him.'

'But what's wrong with them?'

She paused in her sewing, obviously stuck for an answer. 'Nothing. They're just not . . . Bryce's. This is an old-fashioned school, Baz, and it has its little ways. When you're in Rome –'

'What about Rome?'

'Well, you do as the Romans do.'

'What if it means putting up with thugs like Julius Malin?'

'Do you remember reading *Tom Brown's Schooldays*?'

'Nope,' Baz said, rather curtly. He hated admitting that he didn't know things. 'Who's Tom Brown then?'

'Just a boy, in an old book, in a school where the little ones have to run about for the big ones. It was the system in those days, everybody took their turn.'

'That's what Malin told me.'

'It was called "fagging".'

He jerked away from her as she cut the thread, patted his collar and inspected the button. 'Are you saying it's *right* then, this fagging?'

'No, of course not, but this school's been going for hundreds of years, Basil. It has traditions, things get, you know, passed on; I mean, *attitudes* . . .' But her voice trailed into nothing, and she was refusing to meet his eyes. Her case was weak and they both knew it.

He said, 'Well, it's rubbish. I mean, take prefects. They're supposed to make the show run smoothly aren't they, that's all, not going round knocking people about for fun?'

Methodically, without answering the question, she sorted out her sewing-box, winding stray threads round bobbins of cotton, restoring pins to the pincushion. Finding a bit of paper stuck between his teeth, Baz thought again of how Malin had shoved it into his mouth, and of the school election. 'I could run in the head's election, couldn't I?' he said out loud, picking at his teeth. 'I could tell people what *I* think then, about . . . about white shirts, and bullying and this fagging business.'

Calmly The Cow carried on with her tidying. 'You could, but you're a bit new to stick your neck out, if I may say so, and a bit young.'

'*No*. It says anyone can have a go.'

'Oh, well then . . .' and she shrugged.

'Who can stop me?'

'Well, nobody. I can't.' But she was definitely doubtful.

Then an electric bell started yammering very loudly, just outside the door. Baz nearly jumped out of his skin and The Cow consulted her watch. 'Come on, Basil, stir your stumps, you're missing hockey with Mr Slack. Come back on Friday, just so that I can check that lip.' But as he was going to the door, there was a sharp knock and someone stepped inside. Jugsy, the Bat with the Brogues.

Rubbing his hands and with scarcely a glance at Baz, he beamed at The Cow, 'Ah, Matron, I just came to check that Bradshaw had found his way here. A little spot of bother in the playground, you know, nothing more. First day of term, high spirits, etc.,' and he beamed on, but without a shred of warmth or humour in his face.

'You can say that again,' Baz muttered, but not quite low enough. What had happened in the playground was sheer thuggery.

'I beg your pardon?' Jugsy had iced over again and the bland smile had faded to nothing.

'Well, Malin was bullying one of the first years, sir.' Inside Baz was quaking but he was determined to say his piece. 'It's not fair, that's not. He's a prefect too. If I ran this school –'

'Exactly, Bradshaw: if you ran this school. That's what you're going to write about for me, since you obviously have such pronounced views on the subject. *If I ran the school*, three sides, A4, in ink, on my desk tomorrow morning. *Thank you*.' And he turned to go.

'But, sir, what about Julius? He started it.'

'Julius has been seen by Mr Prout, Bradshaw, and what has passed between them is nothing whatever to do with you.'

'But, sir –'

'Shall I make it six sides, Bradshaw, or nine?'

'No, sir.'

'Very well then, thank you for your ministrations, Matron,' and he swept off.

When the door was shut again Baz and The Cow stared at one another. 'Come on,' she said gently. 'Keith Slack'll be wondering where you've got to, if you don't turn up for hockey. You don't want two essays to do this evening, surely?'

'Honestly,' he said with his hand on the doorknob. 'I could just kill some people.'

'Basil, you're late.'

I'm going.

'*OK.*'

6

All the way home Alice prattled on about the wonders of Bryce's and Baz didn't *want* to chat, he'd got too much on his mind. There was the fight for a start, and his cut lip. People had whispered about that, and given him funny looks – and Jugsy obviously wasn't going to let him forget it in a hurry. 'Don't suppose your mother's going to be too thrilled about your face, Bradshaw,' he called out to him, as they'd gone off down the drive. That was wrong. He'd been given a punishment and that ought to be the end of it. But Jugsy did seem to be taking it personally.

Vanessa Honeywell had told him she thought there was something a little bit sad about Jugsy. He lived all on his own and Bryce's school was his life. Last winter, when it had been closed for two weeks because of an oil-tanker strike, Jugsy had come in just the same, every day. He needed it. Baz liked Vanessa, he'd been planning to go the long way home, through Denning where she lived, so they could talk. But Alice had been lying in wait for him outside the cloakrooms and in the end he just couldn't do it to her.

On the bus he told her he thought he might run in the school elections and she was all for it. 'You'd be brilliant, Baz,' she enthused, as they turned into Inkerman Street. 'We could have music and everything, that's what they do at real elections. I could play my trumpet.'

'Hmm.' He wasn't enthusiastic. He'd heard Alice practising, when he'd been for his piano lessons, and it sounded to him as if she'd still got a very long way to go. In an election campaign she could be a bit of a liability. She was too fat for a start. Politicians needed to be surrounded by glamorous women. He said, 'Vanessa Honeywell plays the horn, doesn't she? Wonder if she's any good? I might ask her.'

Alice pouted.

'What's the matter with you, then?'

'Nothing, only it was my idea, Baz, having music.'

'I know it was, I was only saying . . .' But still she pouted, her small pink mouth shrunk to a crumpled line.

'Allie, what's eating you?' But he knew perfectly well, she was jealous of Vanessa Honeywell. She needn't be, though. He couldn't see himself ever accepting the invitation to Vanessa's house. He felt too shy.

'Nothing's eating me. And don't call me Allie, I don't like it,' and she flounced off up the street.

He stared after her for a minute, wondering whether to call her back, then thought better of it, got out his door key and let himself into the house. His mother wouldn't be home from work tonight until six and in the mean time he got busy. First he washed up the breakfast things, then put the casserole she'd left in the oven on a low heat. Then he peeled potatoes and set the table. Finally he settled down to do his punishment essay. He wanted to get it well out of the way before she came home. Pity he couldn't get his lip out of the way. It had swollen up quite a bit during the afternoon and he'd got a dark bruise on his left cheek now where Malin had pushed him. He looked deformed.

He was so engrossed in his essay that he didn't hear her let herself in at the back door. There was only just time to bundle his papers on to the dresser and stick them behind the clock before she was standing over him, frowning and inspecting his face. 'Baz, what have you been up to?'

He didn't answer, just inspected his finger-nails nonchalantly. It was perfectly obvious what he'd been doing, and it wasn't the first time he'd been in a scrap either. There'd been quite a few bullies at the Comp and Baz was a boy who always fought for his rights.

She examined his lip and his bruise. 'Lovey, you've been fighting, haven't you? Oh, Baz . . .'

'Listen, it wasn't my fault, Mum, and I didn't start it, honestly. There was this awful guy, Julius, this Vice-prefect. He was picking on one of the little kids. I couldn't stand it, I just lost my rag.'

'Marvellous,' she said, coldly, turning away to plug in the kettle. 'On your first day, too, when I thought you'd left that sort of thing behind you. Brilliant!'

'Aw, don't Mum. I'm sorry.' He couldn't bear it when she was cold and sarcastic with him. She used to be softer, but she'd changed since they'd lost Dad. He said, 'The matron cleaned my face up, anyhow, and she told me Julius Malin was a bully. She was on my side.' He sniggered. 'Everybody calls her The Cow. It's only because her name's Jersey. She's great.'

'Oh yes,' Mrs Bradshaw said, thawing slightly. 'I remember her at the clothing sale, nice girl.'

'She's a bit vague, though, Mum. This shirt's the wrong colour now, it should be white and you can't wear them with collar buttons, either. Anyhow, I've put it all in this.' He fished out his punishment essay from behind the clock and showed it to her. He was quite proud of his efforts and it had cleared quite a few things up, writing this.

Mrs Bradshaw, always keen to look at his school work, immediately put her glasses on. 'If I ran the school,' she muttered . . . 'For a start – that's not good English, Baz, I'd change that – For a start we wouldn't have any prefects, nobody would be forced to wear uniform if they didn't want to . . . speaking properly isn't the same as talking posh . . . Baz,' she said, suspiciously, eyeing him over the rim of her glasses, 'Is this homework?'

'Well, sort of. What do you reckon? I think it's good.'

'I don't know,' she said doubtfully. 'I suppose "If I ran the school" is a bit more interesting than "What I did on my summer holiday",' and she went on reading. 'Just because you're no good at sport, doesn't mean you're no good. And does Bryce's really need new tennis-courts, especially when it means people losing their jobs? What's that bit about, then?'

'Well, they're not going to build those new houses on

Pullen's Field now. Someone's given Bryce's a lot of money, they've bought it and it's going to be tennis-courts.'

'But, lovey, you've always wanted to learn to play tennis.'

'Mum, that's not the *point*,' Baz said in exasperation. Gee, she could be thick sometimes. 'It's what it means generally, the wildlife will all go, for a start, that's what Ed Pollitt says in our class. Anyhow, Kev's dad's firm was going to do that building job. I shouldn't think he'll be too pleased, will he, if it doesn't go ahead?'

'Really, I'm not sure about this essay, pet,' Mrs Bradshaw muttered, skimming through the pages.

'What's wrong with it?'

'Well, I think it's a bit, you know, *pushy* – from a new boy. I'm not saying you *are* pushy, pet, only that's how it comes over.'

'I'm not changing it, Mum,' he said defiantly, folding his arms. 'It's what I think.' Not only was it what he had decided about Bryce's, it was the beginning of his election campaign. Writing this essay for Jugsy had sorted a lot that was in his mind. He was definitely going to run, and he felt quite excited.

Mrs Bradshaw was fingering his collar. 'I'll have to dig out one of Dad's old ones for tomorrow.' He was silent, then he muttered behind his hand. 'I don't want to wear Dad's things, Mum.'

'I know, but it's only for tomorrow. I can buy you a couple of shirts on Saturday, I'll have been paid.'

She put his essay back behind the clock and glanced at the framed photograph that always stood there now: Baz, Dad and Mum on a Lake District holiday. 'Your Dad would have been proud of you, lovey, getting into Bryce's. Do you know that?'

But Baz didn't reply. He couldn't talk about his father and she knew that. She talked about Dad for her own sake, he decided, not his.

'I'm going upstairs, to take these clothes off.'

'All right, lovey. Tea in twenty minutes.'

Going up to his room he thought about Dad, not at all sure that he'd have approved of Bryce's and all it stood for. And would he have approved of the essay? *If only they could talk.* But where did the dead go? That was the awful thing, the total blankness.

While his mother was listening to The Archers and having a second cup of tea, he slipped next door to see Kev. He'd heard his radio on in the yard. He'd probably be fiddling with his bike. It was always giving trouble when he needed it for his morning paper-round. Mr White had been promising him a new one for months but there was no sign of it yet. He wanted to tell Kev about Julius Malin and to show him his battle scars. Of all people Kev White would sympathize over the fighting. He was rather small and skinny himself and he often got picked on at school. Baz was the one who'd always stood up for him.

'Kev,' he shouted over the fence, above the noise of the radio. 'Want to come over?' The only answer he received was the pop music instantly turned up full volume. He climbed on to the dustbin and peered into the neighbouring yard. Kev had dismantled his brakes and was doing things with a spanner.

'Kev . . . Kev.' If only he'd look at him for a minute. He'd see the bruises then and the lip.

After a minute Kev did look up, but his expression was nothing less than naked loathing. '*You.* Why don't you just drop dead?'

Baz jumped down into the yard. He wasn't afraid of Kev White and someone had to sort him out. 'What's bugging you, Kevin? What's up?'

Kev concentrated on the brakes. 'My dad's gone off, hasn't he?'

'Gone off, where?'

'I dunno. Down the Bay Horse I should think.'

Baz was relieved. 'Oh, is that all? Well, that's nothing new, is it?'

Kev didn't reply but merely went on tinkering with his nuts and screws.

Baz pushed on, determined to get a conversation going. Kev was just being pigheaded, refusing to speak to him because he was going to Bryce's. 'It's OK, isn't it?' he yelled, above the pop music. 'The Bay Horse is his local, isn't it?'

'No, it's *not*, OK! Stick to what you know, Bradshaw.' Kev had come up to the fence and he was brandishing the spanner. Baz backed off slightly. 'Remember how he was before he got his job with Ridgeways? Down there every night till they threw him out? You should know. Your ma banged on the wall enough times. Well there's going to be more banging because he got his cards today. Know why? Because your marvellous new school's bought Pullen's Field for tennis-courts. They've made some filthy deal to get the land. So the building project is *off*. He got a letter this morning, it absolutely stinks. That's the sort of school you're going to. Proud of yourself, are you?' Baz shrank away. 'OK, OK,' he said, 'but Kev it's not my fault, I'm on your side. Listen, we were talking about it in class this morning, Mr Moncrieff – he's my new form teacher – Mr Moncrieff –'

'Oh, Mr Moncrieff-off,' Kev shouted savagely, bashing the rickety fence with his spanner in sheer frustration. 'Get back on your own side, can't you, you're taking up valuable space,' and kicking his tools all over the yard, he went inside and slammed the door behind him.

'Kev . . . *Kev*?' Baz shouted helplessly, but his only answer was the inane quacking of a disc jockey on Radio One.

_____

7

On the bus next morning there was some funny business
over his banana bag. Almost before he'd sat down one of the
Bryce's lot had swiped it, and it was then kicked from row to
row, until he lost sight of it, up at the front. He couldn't go
and get it very easily either, he was squashed into an inside
seat by Alice. Besides, there were too many people standing up,
and the bus conductor was that very bad-tempered woman,
the one who always reported people to Mr Greaves for smoking and for horsing about. Anyhow, he could see Vanessa
Honeywell up at the front; she'd make sure it came back.

He had faith in Vanessa, he'd dreamed about her last
night. They'd gone walking on Darnley Moor together, and
she'd played her French horn to him. It was all getting quite
romantic, when Kev White suddenly ran out from behind
some trees and threw stones at them both, but all the time
he was crying, crying. Baz still felt very mixed up about
Kev, who had pushed past him again this morning, without
speaking; he felt mixed up about going to Bryce's too. Dad
had always said that your worries came out in your dreams.

Alice, who had bagged the seat next to him, the minute
they got on the bus, was too busy studying a book called
Thin is Beautiful to bother much about what was happening
to his bag. 'I'm thinking of going on a diet,' she confided.
'Mummy says she'll do me low-calorie packed lunches for
school, if I want.' Baz glanced at her, getting a whiff of some
rather sickly perfume she was wearing, and noticing that she'd
done her hair differently today, it was all soft and fluffy, quite
pretty for her. She took off her spectacles and rubbed away
the steam. 'I can have contact lenses for my birthday, Daddy

says,' she mused. 'Do you think they'd be better for me, Baz?'

He shrugged. 'Don't know much about contact lenses. Don't they make your eyes water? Any road, don't they cost hundreds of pounds?'

'Well, they *are* expensive. But Daddy says if I really want them . . .'

But Baz wasn't listening any more, he felt nervous. She'd set her sights on him, *definitely*. A diet, contact lenses, new fluffy hair. Alice had always been business-like and organized. She'd got her scholarship at Bryce's through very careful planning. Now she was organizing herself to lose weight, to lure him into her web. It was because she'd twigged that he was interested in Vanessa Honeywell. The passion she'd nursed for him when he'd had those piano lessons was all coming out.

Then a voice said, 'Here's your bag, Baz.' It was *her*, dark and coolly beautiful, and not looking as if she had just pushed her way down a sweaty, steamy bus to give him back his ludicrous banana holdall. (He regretted his frivolous choice of bag now, and his name stencilled in gigantic felt-tip letters all over it. When he'd got the cash he must replace it with something more restrained.)

'Oh, *thanks*.' Even without looking at Alice he could feel a jealous pout from his right.

'That's OK.' Then there was a little silence and neither of them knew what to say next. If only Alice Sugden wasn't sitting there, all four-square, with her diet book and her ears flapping, they could have talked.

'I'd better get back. Someone's saving my seat. Only I thought you'd want your bag. I was just sitting there, and it landed at my feet.' And she was gone down the bus, a slender, glossy-dark vision. She had a smell too, but fresher than Alice's, more countrified. That's where he'd like to be at this moment, walking in the country with Vanessa Honeywell. 'Goody-goody,' grunted Alice sourly, studying the calories in dairy products; but she'd said it just a little too quietly for him to say anything back.

*

He would have thought that Simon Speirs wouldn't have risked it, not after watching that fight with Malin in the playground. But in the form-room, while they were waiting for Jugsy, he had a go at him, about his white shirt, pulling at the collar in that sneering way of his. 'It's a bit *big*, isn't it?' he drawled.

It was. Dad had taken sixteen and a half in shirts, and Baz was only a fourteen. He'd been well aware of the great windy gap round his neck when he put it on this morning, but he'd not liked to say anything. His mother had looked wounded when she'd brought it into his room last night.

'Is this another offering from the Cowshed?' Speirs went on, pretending to examine the quality of the shirt, thrusting his dark, handsome face right up.

Baz heard unconvinced, uneasy laughter from the neighbouring desks and someone, Jake Elder, he thought, actually hissed disapprovingly.

'It was my dad's, if you really want to know.'

'Doesn't he mind you borrowing his clothes? Mine would, he's very fussy.'

Baz raised his voice. 'Wash your ears out Speirs. I said *was*. He can't exactly mind any more, he's *dead*.'

There hadn't been much noise in the form-room before, because people had been listening, as they got their stuff ready for lessons. Now there was absolute silence. Alice whaled in, putting her hand reassuringly on Baz's sleeve, and for once he didn't shake her off. Suddenly, he wanted to cry, about his father, all the crying he'd never done for him, when it had happened. She said, 'Baz's dad was a *hero*, Simon.' And she squeezed his arm.

Baz didn't say anything, he couldn't, but he elbowed Alice gently out of the way and pushed his face right up against Speirs's. The boy retreated, dancing from one foot to the other like a boxer, laughing very loudly, but without humour. He was embarrassed. It was the laughter of someone caught completely off their guard: it was the way Kev had laughed when he'd got home that day and heard his mother had cleared off to Newcastle. It was the laughter of disbelief.

'A *hero*?' he repeated sarcastically. 'I say . . . in the Falklands was he? Or the Gulf?'

Baz grabbed him by the collar. 'Your shirt's too tight, Speirs. Want me to make it a bit tighter — by *strangling you*, for example?' And he tugged at his tie.

'Baz, *Baz*!' screamed Alice, letting out a hysterical squeal.

'Oh, shut up, Alice, and listen, leave my dad out of things in future. Get it? It just causes trouble.'

Now it was Alice who looked ready to burst into tears, and Baz really thought she would have done if the girl on the door hadn't said, 'Jugsy, Jugsy!' in a loud stage whisper. This had the effect of sending everyone to their desks, neatening up their books, pulling ties straight. As the teacher came through the door, Baz glanced across at Simon Speirs. He had a silly, floppy sort of look now, he had definitely not liked the hiss of disapproving laughter, and if he'd not been dark-skinned, he would surely have been blushing. Baz decided he'd won against Squeaky Clean, this round, anyhow.

Jugsy hadn't improved overnight. Here he was again, bald head polished to a high gloss, pink hands rubbing obsessively together, issuing the same staccato commands. 'Good morning, 3M. Sit. Number off if you please.' No change, except for an unscheduled ferocious bark at Jake Elder, who didn't deliver his number on time. He was too busy drawing a geometric design of amazing complexity on a pad, and filling in hundreds of tiny squares with illegal felt-tip pens.

Snapping the register shut, Jugsy called for the punishment essays. 'Edward Pollitt, *Disobedience*; James Elder, *Insolence* and *The mindless majority*, and Basil Bradshaw . . . ah yes, Bradshaw, *If I ran the school*.' He spoke very slowly and deliberately, clearly wanting the full horror of the various crimes to be felt by the class. Nobody reacted much though, except that there was faint laughter from somewhere when Baz's title was read out.

'It's not funny, Pearson,' he rapped, tapping the side of his nose. 'Right, the essays please.'

Jake ambled up first and dumped a handful of rather tatty-looking sheets on the desk. Then Polly bounded out of his seat and placed a neatly-typed essay on top of Jake's.

'*Thank you*, Pollitt. You've been word processing, I see. My, oh my. Now then, Bradshaw, your plans for a better world, please . . .' And the pink fingers uncurled, expectantly.

But Baz couldn't find his essay. 'Come on, Mr Bradshaw. We have things to do this morning,' snapped Jugsy impatiently.

'It's here somewhere, sir,' Baz muttered, foraging deep into the red bag. 'Oh, yeah, it's here, got it . . .' and he leapt from his seat and ran to the front with it, jubilant somehow, forgetting it was a punishment. He couldn't help feeling proud of what he'd written.

'Thank you, Bradshaw, and wipe that silly smile off your face will you? It's not everybody who can get a serious imposition on their first day, at one of the best schools in the country.'

Baz didn't speak, merely sagged a little as Jugsy snatched the essay from him. 'Did you hear what I said, Bradshaw?'

'Yes, sir.'

'Well then, take note. And what about your hair? I told you to get it cut. You too, Elder, I told you both quite distinctly and neither of you has been near a barber. That's perfectly obvious.'

'My mum had a go at it, sir,' Baz muttered in embarrassment, 'after the shops were shut. I didn't have enough money to go to the barber's.'

'I didn't either, sir,' Jake called out. Jugsy stared at the unruly orange mop with distaste. There seemed more of it than yesterday. The boy had obviously washed it on purpose, then bushed it up to look even wilder.

'Oh sit *down*, Elder,' he said tetchily. 'I'll give you both until Monday morning to get your hair seen to, and that's my absolute deadline. By the way, Bradshaw, don't roll your essays up in future. This isn't exactly the Magna Carta, you know. Now then, let's see how you plan to rule the world, shall we?' and he flattened out the essay.

Baz returned to his place, hating him for his pernickety obsession with hair, and with whether or not an essay should be rolled or folded, like wrapping-paper . . . But, wait a minute, he'd *not* rolled it. And where had that rubber band come from that was holding it together? Suddenly, he thought of that larking about with his bag on the bus. Had someone interfered with his stuff, then?

They evidently had, because Jugsy was reading through the curling sheets giving off little snorts, his mouth set in a grim line. 'Who is responsible for this? You, Elder, you're the artist among us?' And he held up Baz's neatly-written pages one by one. Across each, in large thick black letters, was scrawled VOTE FOR BAZ.

Jake got to his feet without being asked. He was at a crucial stage with his pattern but this accusation was too much. '*Me*, sir?' he spluttered indignantly. 'How can it be anything to do with me? Anyhow, what's it on about, "Vote for Baz"?'

'I really have no idea, Elder, but I intend to find out. Bradshaw, have you any idea who could have done this to your essay?'

Baz hesitated, remembering the bus. Had Julius Malin been on it, or had he got the earlier one? There'd been a very big crowd and he'd not seen him. Kev had been there, though, with Alex Brodey, *and* Simon Speirs. Perhaps they'd all been talking about this school election thing. Perhaps Speirs had told them this new boy was going in for it. It was funny, how things got out. He must have listened, when Polly was discussing it all with Baz. Simon Speirs was a *spy*. He'd definitely been around. He said, deliberately avoiding the question, 'It was OK when I put it in my bag this morning, sir.'

'Don't say OK. I see. So whoever did this, this *thing*, could have done it on the bus. You do travel by bus, Bradshaw?'

'I do.'

It was becoming like a trial in a courtroom drama, the judge in his funeral black, the accused sagging before him, everyone else listening hard; and he'd not *done* anything, for Heaven's sake.

'And did you have your school-bag with you at *all times*?'

'No, sir, people were sort of larking about, you know, and it ended up at the front. I got it back though, sir.'

'Evidently. But your ability to look after your personal possessions is unimpressive, Bradshaw. Boys will be boys, you know, and of course, girls will be girls. Now, I really can't waste time on a fruitless investigation of who came to deface your essay, on or off the bus. You will simply have to write it all out again.'

'But, *sir* . . .' Baz began.

'However,' interrupted Jugsy, 'before we get on to more important things, what is it about, this voting business?'

'Well, it's the school election, isn't it, sir?' Baz replied in a tight and furious little voice. Fancy having to do it *again*, when it wasn't his *fault*! And he knew who'd done it, Speirs, who was studiously poring over a list of Latin verbs, pretending not to listen to what was going on. It had to be Speirs. He'd got that look on his face.

'I don't know.' Jugsy said. 'Is it?'

'Well, I'm going in for it, aren't I?'

'Are you?' At this exchange there was laughter, mainly from the Squeaky Clean boys and from Speirs. 'Oh, do stop talking in that silly way, Bradshaw,' snapped Jugsy.

'What's silly about it, sir?'

The question, though innocently intended, clearly struck Jugsy as outrageously rude. He went white and clenched his clean pink fingers into knots, barely able to contain himself. 'Bradshaw,' he said, 'let's talk plain English, please. Are you telling me you intend to take part in the school election?'

'Yes, sir. There's no age limit, I've looked on the notices. It's not just for prefects, it sez.'

'*Sez*. While you're at it,' Simon Speirs muttered, to no one in particular, turning over a page of his verb tables, 'why don't you invest in a few grammar lessons; we don't have illiterates at Bryce's. And why do you have to look like a golliwog?'

Powerless, Baz wanted to thump him. They both had the same kind of wiry, woolly hair, but Speirs's was clipped terribly short and neat, as if he was somehow denying himself, denying his origins. Once, way back, Dad's ancestors had been slaves. This boy's too, perhaps. Why couldn't they talk? When Baz had first seen him he'd actually thought they might become friends, with their similar backgrounds. It had clearly been a ludicrous hope.

'I see. Well, if those are the rules I can't prevent you, Bradshaw. But before you buckle down to your all-important election speech, perhaps, as I've already said, you'd be good enough to rewrite this essay, in ink, please, for tomorrow morning. You really can't expect me to accept a mess like this, now can you? Here you are, go on, take it.'

'But *sir*,' Baz protested, 'that's not fair, it wasn't me who wrote all over it.'

'I beg your *pardon*, Bradshaw,' Jugsy said icily, in tones of exaggerated horror. 'In this school you are responsible for your *own* property at *all* times. It's in the Rule Book. Now then, perhaps you'd like me to add a few extra pages on "Carelessness"? Would you? Answer me, Bradshaw!'

'No, sir.' Taking the ruined essay he slunk back to his place, hating the school, the election, most of all Simon Speirs. Vanessa, from her front seat, gave him a heart-warming little smile as he passed by and Alice whispered. 'Never mind, Baz, it's all . . . silly.'

'Oh, *don't*,' he muttered as he sat down, a great gloom sweeping over him. He should never have taken a scholarship to this place, it was awful.

As Jugsy turned to the blackboard and started squeaking away with the chalk, Simon Speirs, for all his superior airs and graces, blew a quiet but definite raspberry.

*

68

People were very sympathetic about Baz's ruined essay, even Jake, who'd been accused by Jugsy, and at break in the playground he found himself in the middle of rather an admiring crowd. This was reassuring, anyhow. He'd always tended to be in the centre of things at the Comp. He just seemed to draw people. Mum said that was what he needed to watch, getting big-headed.

'I thought Simon Speirs was up to something,' Alice said with authority, edging up very close to Baz as usual. 'I just had that feeling when he got on the bus, you know.'

'Well, why didn't you tell me, *twit*,' muttered Baz grumpily. People laughed and Alice immediately pouted, flushing pale beetroot. 'Well, it was just a *feeling*, Baz, that's all.'

'Honestly, I could smash his great ugly face in.' He said it very loudly, hoping someone who was nearby, with the Squeaky Cleans, might hear.

'Oh don't be ridiculous. You can't go around *accusing* people, when you've no proof. My mother says —'

'*Dry up about your mother, Alice!*' Baz yelled. Suddenly, he was quite furious with her. Why did she have to embarrass him all the time? The little crowd fell silent. Alice shrank away and he realized he'd gone too far, bellowing at her like that. But she did get on his nerves, wittering on about her mother.

'Is that going into your election speech then, Baz?' asked Polly, pleasantly enough, but with just a hint of mockery.

'What do you mean?'

'*How to Run the School*: (a) beat everyone up, (b) scream at people when they are just trying to help, (c) accuse people of —'

'Of course not. I was just saying, I mean ... Listen ... Sorry, Alice.'

'It's OK.' But you could tell she was hurt. She had retreated now and was standing next to Vanessa. They seemed quite friendly. They were even linking arms.

Baz wanted to be on good terms with Polly, he was his own

man, he rather admired him. He said, feeling very foolish, after his burst of bad temper, 'I just meant, you know, well, Simon . . . Listen, are you going in for this election thing?'

'Oh yes, well, *of course*. Vote for Polly, friends, Vote Green. Others will promise the moon, only the Greens can guarantee the Earth.'

'You're a cheat, Pollitt, that was on the leaflet,' grunted Jake Elder. 'Anyhow, nobody can guarantee the Earth, the Earth's had it.'

Polly took no notice, he was obviously more interested in Baz. 'Did you read my leaflet?' he said, staring at him with his wide-awake blue eyes.

'Yes, last night.' He'd been in bed falling asleep but he had looked at it. It made sense too. He thought it would have appealed to Dad.

'*Green,*' he heard. 'Go Green, huh. He must be colour-blind!' This was Simon Speirs talking to his Squeaky Clean friends, and Baz was most definitely meant to hear.

They weren't the only people interested in the election, it seemed. Something was going on in another part of the playground, something very noisy, involving a ghetto blaster and a lot of people standing on chairs singing. On a tall laboratory stool, several inches higher than anyone else, a boy was shouting through a rolled-up newspaper which he was using as a megaphone. 'This is the Cliff Richard Revival Party speaking and I'm asking you to vote for me in the school elections. Come on, *move* it fans!' Someone turned the machine up very loud and they suddenly heard 'Congratulations and Celebrations' echoing all over the yard.

Instinctively Baz looked round for the duty master. It was Keith Slack, the fat one with the purple track suit, the friendly laid-back PE teacher who'd taken them yesterday for hockey. He did not really seem bothered when Baz had turned up fifteen minutes late, just told him to join the others and been delighted when he'd scored a goal. He'd smelt of beer and cigarettes and he was smoking now. He'd only stayed in the yard for five minutes and then cleared off. Baz could see him puffing away out on one of the playing-fields.

He stared at the boy on the stool. 'It's incredible,' he whispered to Polly, as the noisy, giggling group drifted towards them. 'He looks like Cliff Richard, I mean he honestly *does*.'

'I know, his name's Clifford Turner. He *says* his mum and dad called him after *the* Cliff, but I don't know if it's true.'

'Mine had all his records,' Baz said nostalgically, thinking of the old days. 'They were both mad on Cliff Richard. It's a bit old-fashioned now though, isn't it?'

'Oh, I think it's cool. Cliff'll get votes. He's popular.'

Clifford Turner was gyrating luxuriously to the music, using his newspaper as a mike now, leading a large though obviously rather bashful crowd in the chorus of 'Congratulations'. He didn't really look all that much like Cliff Richard, now Baz had got a closer look, though he did have smooth dark hair, a tan (surely out of a tube?) and extremely white teeth. He was also wearing sun-glasses, and he'd swapped his school blazer for a denim waistcoat. Intrigued, Baz went up to him.

'You serious then, about reviving Cliff Richard?'

'Sure I'm serious. Wanna join my party?' They'd moved on to 'Living Doll', now, and Cliff was bopping about rather more slowly and sexily.

'No. No, I don't think so. I'm running my own y'see.'

Clifford shrugged. 'OK. Suit yourself.' And he turned back to his audience. 'Join the Cliff Richard Revival Party!' he bellowed again, through his newspaper megaphone. 'Cliff Richard, with more hits than anyone in history except Elvis. Think what he's done for this country folks, think of all the cash he's brought in to prop up the economy. "Age cannot wither him, nor custom stale his infinite variety", as the Bard says. Vote for Cliff, he's the Queen Mother of pop music. He'll go on for ever!'

Someone had turned the ghetto blaster up to maximum and the distorted, vibrating smoochings of 'Living Doll' filled the playground. There was a very large crowd now, all swaying

71

to the conducting of Clifford. Some of the girls had their eyes closed. They were screaming and falling about, others were laughing and sniggering. In the general din nobody noticed Jugsy, whose polished pink dome suddenly popped up by the rocking laboratory stool. Snatching the newspaper megaphone, he crumpled it up furiously, then snapped off the ghetto blaster.

'How dare you,' he spluttered, 'how dare you make this disgusting racket in the middle of the recreation period. Get off that stool, Turner, and restore your blazer to its rightful place if you please. Are you out of your mind? Oh no, I'll take that.'

His scrubbed pink fingers closed on the shiny black and chrome ghetto blaster and thrust it under one arm, where it disappeared into the folds of his academic gown.

'But, sir,' Clifford Turner protested, rather feebly, clambering off his stool. 'It's a musical instrument, and I need it, for my campaign.'

'What campaign, Turner?'

'The Cliff Richard Revival Party, sir, I'm running it. Want to join, sir?' he added slyly. The listening crowd gasped.

'Don't be impertinent, Turner. This machine is confiscated. You may collect it from the office at 4 o'clock. As for your silly campaign –'

'Sir,' Baz interrupted boldly. 'It's not silly, he's just running a fringe group, y'know, like the Monster Raving Loonies. Elections always have them.'

'Silence, Bradshaw! When I want your opinion I'll ask for it. Now where on earth is Mr Slack?'

'On the field, sir,' Simon Speirs informed him, quick as a whip. Baz was sickened. According to Polly there'd been some kind of a bust-up between Simon Speirs's uncle and Mr Slack one parents' night the uncle was said to have called him a 'fat slob', and people said he'd been taking it out on Simon ever since. Here was a chance to get him into more trouble. Baz could tell that Jugsy didn't approve either of the overweight chain-smoking PE teacher, who followed the cross-country runners on his motor bike.

'Well, kindly tell him he's needed *here*, Speirs, at *once*. Go on, hurry up. Now then, what's this . . .' Turning on his heel, Jugsy was now bearing down upon another very noisy group, at the far end of the playground. 'Miss Weatherall, what on earth are *you* doing? And is that litter I see? Pick it up girl, or I'll put you into detention. Did you know there are national fines imposed these days, for the dropping of litter?'

'No, sir, sorry, sir. I'll pick it up at once, sir.'

'Yes, sir, no, sir, three bags full, sir,' Jugsy repeated sarcastically. 'What are you *doing*, Harriet Weatherall, and what have you got in that bag?'

Jugsy was somehow turning into a bad-tempered Pied Piper. As he'd stalked across the playground, everyone had drifted after him. Nobody wanted to miss anything. Harriet Weatherall from 4B was an absolute scream.

There she was, distributing small cheerfully-wrapped packages to the juniors, and they were ripping the Cellophane off and stuffing the contents into their mouths. 'Let's put the "Great" back into Britain, fans,' she was yelling. 'Eat more jelly! Come on, you lot, it's free!'

'Miss Weatherall . . . Harriet . . . please stop *screaming* like that. Now, what's all this about, for Heaven's sake?' Harriet Weatherall was rather comical to look at, gawky and tall, with a great hooked nose and with a frizz of yellow hair. Her blouse was unbuttoned half-way down, her tie was undone and she was surely wearing make-up. She was just not 'Bryce's'. Baz's heart went out to her at once. She was another loony fringe person, giving out her packets of jelly and the little ones obviously adored her. This was great. He was going to enjoy the school election if it had people like Harriet and Clifford in it. Getting close he caught a jelly packet and proceeded to unwrap it.

'Bradshaw,' Jugsy thundered, 'put that down!' Baz obediently dropped the jelly on the asphalt. 'No, not there, I meant — oh, give it to me.'

'Here, sir, there's plenty. Roll up, roll up, everyone. *Eat more jelly!* Let's put the "Great" back in Great Britain, shall we?' Harriet's nose swept this way and that as she enticed her diminutive supporters with the lure of food. She took no notice whatever of Jugsy's apoplectic protests. She was irrepressible.

'You can't *sell* things, Weatherall,' he was saying rather helplessly as people dived for the jelly. 'We have a perfectly adequate tuck-shop on the school premises.'

'I'm not selling it, sir. It's free. It's from my uncle's cash and carry. Best quality. Do you want some?'

'*NO I DO NOT!* Attend to your clothing, Harriet, and then go and wash all that muck off your face, it's strictly against the rules. You're a disgrace to the school. Ah, Mr Slack . . . thank goodness.'

'More jelly, anyone?' Harriet whispered, with a grin, as the two teachers put their heads together, turning their backs momentarily on the crowd. Baz giggled.

'Don't think she'll make it, somehow,' Polly said to him, as the bell rang for the end of break and they joined the general surge towards the school buildings. 'Don't think Clifford Turner will either. I can't honestly see him talking to the whole school.'

'Why not? He's good.'

'Yes, but he'd be nervous. He gets nervous about everything. Goes to pieces in exams, he's that type. Pity. This dump could do with livening up a bit.'

Baz was thoughtful. 'Do you think it's just a big laugh then, this election? I thought you were going to run for the Greens, I thought you were serious – and by the way, how have you worked out that *I'm* Green? I never said I was.'

'Well, it sounded like it yesterday,' said Polly, 'when you were talking to Jugsy about not having any more tennis-courts. That's a conservation issue.'

'Yes,' argued Baz, 'but it doesn't mean I'm *Green*. I don't want labels stuck on me, thanks very much.'

'OK, OK,' Polly said good-naturedly. 'Just thought we might have something in common, that's all. What are you going to campaign for then? And what are you going to call yourself? The name is very important. I mean I've got one ready made. It's national,' he said proudly.

'Dunno, yet. I want things to be a bit fairer in this place, for a start. I don't like a system that lets the little ones get bullied. All that rubbish about school uniforms too, I'd put an end to that, straight away. What do you think?'

It had occurred to Baz that this might be his line, a kind of people's charter for the pupils of Bryce's school. He could raise issues that affected people *directly*. Saving the whale and recycling rubbish, making your own compost and taking stuff to the bottle-bank was all very well, but really it was more for adults. People were selfish, they would vote for things that were going to affect *them*. Dad had always said that. 'It's the cry of humanity,' he had once told Baz. 'What about *me*?'

'Well, what *do* you think?' he repeated. Polly he thought was looking rather embarrassed.

The other boy hesitated. 'Well, I honestly don't think you are going to win an election on white shirts and bullying. I don't mean to sound rude but, you know, you've got to think nationally, internationally . . . *cosmically*. That's why I'm Green, you see, it involves the whole planet. I think you should join up with me. I bet we'd win then, hands down. My power and influence and your . . . pzazz,' and he waved his hands expansively. 'Vote for Baz, he's got PZAZZ.'

'I've got what?'

'You know, *IT*.'

'Oh, you mean sex appeal?' Baz said hopefully, thinking of Vanessa.

'Well, yes, that's part of it, I'd say you'd got that, and you need it in an election. Look at how the real politicians do it, they spend thousands on getting expert advice, on how to present themselves, on how they look and speak. And the point is, at the moment, there are more girls at Bryce's than boys, so any guy worth looking at has got a head start, and you definitely *are*. You should hear some of the girls going on about you. Now look at me, Mr Universe, what chance have I got?'

Baz did look, and he could see what the modest Polly was getting at. He was wispy and thin with muscles like knots on cotton, built like Kev White, but a bit taller, and he had a piping, high voice, which wouldn't help when he had to make election speeches. No, he'd have hard work, running his campaign all on his own, in spite of his obvious brainpower.

'I liked it when you punched Julius Malin in the face,' Polly went on, inspecting his pathetic muscles rather gloomily. 'He's the biggest creep in the school. Everyone can see it, except the headmaster. A lot of people have been wanting to do that for a long time, but you did it, on your first day. Now I'm not saying I approve of violence, I don't, I'm a pacifist. But I did take my hat off to you for doing that. I thought, "Here's a guy I can talk to." *So*, think about coming in with me, I'm serious.'

'I'm not sure,' Baz muttered, following him into school under the archway, though he was certainly very flattered by what Polly had said, if he was sincere (and you could never really tell with people, his father had said that). It was true that he was rather good to look at, seemed to have something about him that attracted people. It had at the Comp, anyhow. Mum was always doing him down a bit on that score. 'Remember you're *human*,' she told him now and again. It was what the Emperor's servants had whispered to him in one of their fairy stories, when Baz was a little kid. She still loved him though; and Dad had loved him.

Jake, Alice and Vanessa had been listening to Polly's advice to Baz. The five of them seemed to be forming a definite group now, against the Squeaky Cleans, Baz hoped; and now the lustrous Vanessa was offering to help him as well. 'I'd vote for you, Baz,' she was saying. 'I could get you some stuff too, if you like, for your campaign.'

'Really? What kind of stuff?'

'Well, my dad owns Orlando, you know, it's that boutique in the new shopping precinct. He's got three of them. He sells T-shirts and badges that people can decorate themselves, that kind of thing. I'm sure I could get him to give me some of the "imperfects", he has loads. We could wear them for the campaign, and we could give people badges, you know, like Harriet's jelly.'

'Great, that'd be *great*,' Baz said. 'Could I come and talk to your dad, do you think, could I ring him? I mean, we'd need some money, wouldn't we?' and they disappeared under the arch together chatting busily.

'Vote for Baz, he's got pzazz!' screeched Jake Elder, running after them, but Alice stayed exactly where she was, in the playground. She'd been listening to Baz and Vanessa and she looked completely crushed, almost wounded; her whole plump body sagged.

'Come on, Alice,' Polly said kindly, turning back. 'It's history next and Mr Banerjee will lose his rag if we are late. You can always join the Greens, you know, you could help me. You'd be welcome.'

'Oh, *shut up*,' she hissed at him through clenched teeth. Polly shrugged. Baz Bradshaw's bad mood was obviously catching this morning.

'Sorry I spoke,' he muttered in a hurt voice, loping off towards history. 'I was only trying to *help*.'

8

Nobody could quite make their minds up, about Baz Bradshaw; he could tell, and it hurt. People were reasonably friendly towards him, but somehow, with the exception of Vanessa and the loyal Alice, they all kept a certain distance. He wasn't even sure about Polly, and everyone seemed to like *him*, in spite of his endless boring on about the Green issue. He was so easygoing you couldn't *not* like him. But what was it, about Baz himself?

Was it that he'd made a big impact with his first election meeting? He'd attracted big crowds, certainly, with his speeches, and they'd been amazed when he'd turned up in a pair of Mum's ear-rings. Jugsy had soon got rid of *those*, of course.

Also, he'd decided, it must be because he was clever. They had weekly mark-readings at Bryce's. Each Thursday morning, Jugsy read out every single mark you'd got that week, in all subjects; the marks were then added up, an average worked out and form positions given. Then, in Prayers on the Friday, Slime read out the top and bottom three names in each class. It was awful if you'd done very badly; sometimes the little ones cried. After a couple of weeks Baz found himself in the top three; after another week he was first, and he stayed there. He wasn't a swot, he just found the work easy and he liked it, even Latin and German, which he'd never done before. At Jugsy's mark-reading, the first time he came top, Polly whispered loudly that marks like Basil Bradshaw's were 'disgusting' and shouldn't be allowed. But he seemed to be saying it as a joke, at least that was what Baz preferred to think. Anyhow, *he* was near the top in all the sciences, and in Maths, so Baz really didn't threaten him. Simon Speirs was a much bigger problem, he *was* a swot, and before Baz had joined the class, he'd nearly always come top himself. In view of his general hostility, and that of the Squeaky Clean people he'd now gathered round him, it would have been better if Baz had done really badly in something, on purpose. But you couldn't *do* that. He came to dread Jugsy's mark-reading though. Speirs and Co. always whispered about him afterwards.

He found he was one of the best at sport too, and this just made things worse. Every time he went out on the hockey field he decided he'd keep in the background, but he was a winger, so how could he? The centre-half always passed the ball to him, knowing he was good, and could get it up the field faster than anyone else. What was he supposed to do? Deliberately miss it?

Swimming was no help either. Baz had learned to swim when he was a baby, because Dad had once swum for the county and was determined to teach him as soon as he was out of nappies. So by seven or eight he'd already started winning little competitions. Less than a fortnight after he'd come to Bryce's, Keith Slack put him into the school squad, even though everyone else in it was a senior. And in the spring term they were going in for a big national school's championship. It was going on TV.

His mother was very proud of everything, especially the swimming, knowing how it would have pleased Dad. She didn't really understand how being Bryce's Golden Boy caused problems, or why he didn't bring his new friends home. The one teacher that seemed to have an inkling about the situation was Keith Slack, who sometimes chatted to him in the changing rooms after hockey practice, when the others had gone. He obviously knew about Dad; he never mentioned what had happened, just said once, 'I sometimes used to have a drink with your father, Basil, at the County Baths after our training sessions. Fine man.' It was enough.

His only opportunity to act the fool was in music. He wasn't exactly tone-deaf, but those piano lessons with Alice's mother had been a trial. For a start he had very big hands, with thick stubby fingers, no good at all for playing 'Fairy Revels' and the niminy-piminy pieces Mrs Sugden seemed to favour. He liked the music lessons at Bryce's too, they were so relaxing after the relentless pen-pushing you got with people like Jugsy, Mr Banerjee and Dr Prout. 'Granny' Baxter, the elderly teacher who'd come out of retirement for a term to stand in for the regular head of music, who'd just had a big operation, was a plump, white-haired, motherly old soul, like everyone's favourite gran, and they never did very much work with her, just 'singing' if you could call it that, and listening to tapes. Sometimes people brought their instruments and played, with Granny Baxter accompanying them on the piano. Baz was amazed to discover that Simon Speirs could play the flute brilliantly. It was hard to believe that such fantastic music could come from the hands of such a creep, and Vanessa wooed them all too, on her French horn. Baz felt a bit jealous, and somehow underprivileged. He was doing well in lessons because he'd been born with a fair amount of grey matter between his ears. But musical instruments were something different again, these people had obviously been playing them for years and years. He definitely felt out of it in music, and grumpy with his parents for not starting him off early on something. It had been too late by the time he'd had those piano lessons with Mrs Sugden. Mum was right, he *did* want to shine in everything. Was that why people kept their distance?

Alice always cheered him up though. In spite of the celebrated Mr Gordon, who was now giving her lessons in school, she really wasn't very good, yet, on her trumpet, and sometimes her attempts to get the very high notes turned into a series of manic squeaking noises. 'Very *good*, dear,' soothed Granny Baxter, but her soft voice never covered up the giggles and snorts from the class. 'It's a difficult instrument to play,' she would add encouragingly, frowning vaguely at the gigglers.

'Especially when you are fifteen stone.' This was Simon Speirs, carefully inspecting his flute. Baz did loathe him, but after his burst of bad temper at the beginning of term he was doing his absolute best to be patient with Alice. There *was* something in what Speirs said though, her *Thin is Beautiful* book didn't seem to be having the desired effect, in fact she seemed to be expanding. Was it 'comfort eating', he thought, guiltily, because he was getting more and more friendly with Vanessa?

It was Granny Baxter and the music lessons that helped him with his election campaign. After a month, apart from the loony people and Baz's own group, two major parties had emerged, though nothing official had happened yet and he still had time to plan how to go about things. The two main groups were Polly's Greens and the Malin–Speirs 'Squeaky Clean' party, headed by Malin because he was the senior. They called themselves 'CA', which apparently meant 'Cut Above'.

Baz never spoke to Speirs if he could help it, but he found out what CA stood for, from Polly. 'Cut Above' was the name of a very expensive men's hairdressing salon in Darnley town centre and to Malin and Co. things like neat hair, smart dress, and highly-polished shoes were all-important. Not only did they want to maintain school uniform at Bryce's, they actually wanted to tighten up on it, Malin's point being that your *appearance* reflected the person you were *inside*. Baz had heard him going on about this one day in the playground, though he had pretended not to be listening of course. 'Sloppy presentation means sloppy thinking,' was what he had actually said, and then, 'This school is going to produce people who will be leaders in their field. OK let them look and sound like leaders. Vote for Cut Above! We'll get you there!' How people spoke was another thing he seemed obsessed with. Polly said he'd actually suggested elocution lessons, for those in the school with 'speech problems'. Baz was very suspicious about this. It was the local accent that Malin didn't like, not bad speech, and the rot had started with his friend in 3M, Simon Speirs, who'd mocked the way Baz spoke, that first day in the bus queue. Malin was all for tightening up the prefect system too. He didn't think that discipline at Bryce's was strict enough.

'In other words, keep everything exactly as it is, but worse?' Baz said gloomily to Polly, when he heard the low-down on the Cut Above campaign.

'More or less. They are the school Conservatives, I suppose.'

'*Preservatives*, I'd say. Hey, why don't they call themselves "The Fossils"? They are as good as, they're dead.'

'Fossils . . . fossils . . .' Polly had played with the word like chewing-gum before spitting it out. '*No*, it's not got the ring of success, somehow.'

'Well, neither has Cut Above if you ask me. It'll just attract the snobs, that will.'

'Hmm. That may well be part of it. There are quite a few snobs around, Baz.'

'Yes. I've noticed. A name's very important though, isn't it? I'm still thinking about mine. Wish I could decide.'

He eventually got it from a music lesson, which was also memorable for something else; it happened on the day that 3M behaved so badly for Granny Baxter that she actually cried. It was awful.

Her problem was that she never waited for quiet first, before starting a lesson, but plunged straight in, while people were still fooling about, vainly hoping that the lovely music she was planning to put on for them might calm things down. But it never did. Simon Speirs, a real goody-goody in most people's lessons, was down on the floor at the back of the class, playing poker with some of his friends, when she walked in.

'Aw, come *on*,' Baz whispered, breaking his rule to speak to them. Granny B. looked so upset. Alice stuck up for him. She really wasn't afraid of anybody. 'Yes, get *up*, Simon,' she ordered him in her bossiest voice. 'You're being really rotten, and she let you play your flute last week. It's a shame.'

'Push off, banana boy,' Speirs said, ignoring Baz completely and dealing another hand, 'and take your fat friend with you. There's a bad smell around here.'

Polly, who was very fond of Granny B. and never fooled around for her even though he did in other lessons, grabbed a pair of cymbals from the percussion corner and clashed them together. 'Order! Order!' he yelled. It sounded just like that man in the Houses of Parliament, except that people there didn't seem to listen to him. Polly got 3M quiet though. Baz was almost certain he saw him give Simon Speirs a sly kick in the backside, then glare at him, daring him not to respond to Granny B. Whatever happened it did the trick and the poker players took their seats rather sheepishly, just in time to hear Granny B. introducing Beethoven's Fifth Symphony.

'Not all of us can respond to classical music, dears,' she was clucking benignly, beaming across at Simon as if he'd been sitting there all the time, 'but I'm sure everybody will recognize *this* piece. And of course, although Beethoven was German, and we were fighting Germany when this became really famous, it was our victory sign in the Second World War.' She laughed, 'Not that any of *you* were around at the time.'

'I was, miss,' murmured Jake Elder. 'But then I'm a walking miracle.'

If Granny B. heard this, and the laughter that followed, she pretended not to, because the next minute she was letting Jake put the tape on for her. The splendid quadraphonic hi-fi system was brand-new, a present from the Parents' Association, and she admitted that she didn't understand its workings yet.

Baz felt anxious for her as he watched Jake, grinning broadly, fiddling with the knobs and switches. There had been something a bit too eager about his offer and he'd got that *look* on his face. Jake Elder was a joker, but he never knew when to stop. He'd got two detentions this term already, for cheek, and those were only the ones Baz knew about. And soon enough he understood what he was up to.

'OK, Mrs Baxter,' Jake was saying, slipping a tape into position, 'it's all ready to go. You just press that button, and you're away.'

'Thank you, dear. Now then, settle down to listen, everyone, this really is the most famous symphonic opening in the world,' and she hummed the first cadences softly, in an even, surprisingly sweet voice, 'da, da, da, *da* . . .' as she pressed the button.

'Congratulations', sung fortissimo by Cliff Richard, echoed round the room. Jake had swapped tapes, turned the powerful system up to full volume, and the whole place was vibrating with it. At first people looked surprised, then they dissolved into titters, and started clapping their hands along with Jake, who'd climbed up on to his desk and was doing a Cliff, smooching sexily over a non-existent mike, his mad orange hair flopping about shaggily as he bopped rhythmically to and fro.

Granny Baxter was bewildered, and she clearly couldn't stand the enormous booming noise. 'Stop it. Oh, *stop it*, somebody,' she begged tearfully, clapping her hands over her ears. 'That really was *very* naughty, when I asked you to start the Beethoven. Now why go and do a thing like that? And get off the desk, you silly boy, before you fall off and hurt yourself.'

Someone on the front row leaned forward and clicked off the machine and there was miraculous quiet. But Jake, as he clambered down, was still vaguely bopping about and still grinning. He was obviously very pleased with himself.

'It's one of the election tunes, Mrs Baxter,' he explained. 'We're all having music you see. I mean, you've *got* to have music.'

'I don't know what you are talking about.' Granny Baxter's gentle voice had become all strangled suddenly and she'd turned very red.

'Well, it's the tune for the Cliff Richard Revival Party. I'm their agent in this class. Do you want to join? I can get you a badge.'

'No, *of course* I don't want to join. This is a music lesson, a *serious* music lesson, and I'd planned for us to have a really lovely time together. Now you've spoiled it with your stupidity, I don't ... I don't ... oh, I wish you'd not done that, Peter, Jonathan ... whatever your name is, what *is* your name?' She was crying.

'Jake Elder, miss. Aw listen, I'm sorry. I never meant – listen, I'll put on the Beethoven straight away.'

'No. I'm not sure I want it now. You have to be in the mood for great music and you've spoiled everything. It was going to be so nice. Do what you like all of you, I'm finished for this morning. I'm sorry,' and she sat down and wiped her eyes.

There was an appalled silence, and everyone stared at Jake, who was now absolutely scarlet. He whispered helplessly to a thunderous-looking Polly, who was sharing his double desk, 'Listen, mate, it was only a bit of fun ...' But you could tell that the whole form was hating him. A complete change of tack was called for.

Baz put his hand up. 'Miss?'

Granny B. sniffed, 'Yes dear? Can it wait? I'm not really in the mood for silly questions.'

'Miss, it's not silly, it's about the election, miss.'

Mrs Baxter composed herself and looked at him. 'You're new aren't you? Do I know your name?'

'Baz Bradshaw.'

She stroked her chin thoughtfully. 'Bradshaw ... *Bradshaw* ... Ah, yes, I remember, we were told in the staff meeting. That terrible thing at the building society. Oh, my dear ...' He was near enough to touch and she stretched out a hand. Baz shrank away, horrified that she might gather him to her bosom or something; that was the sort of motherly person she was. He said hurriedly, 'It's just that I'm going in for this election campaign, you see, and I wondered – have you any music *I* could use?'

She brightened at once. This seemed like a genuine, serious enquiry and the class, overawed by her sudden tears, had settled down and were being as quiet as mice. 'Well, let's see. What's the name of your party, dear?'

'I've not really decided yet. I just call it BAZ. It's, y'know, all very basic stuff, about how I think we should start running the school, equal rights for people, no prefect system, freedom of speech, and a school council, so that *everyone* can say what they think. It's quite popular,' he added proudly. 'Lots of people come to my meetings.'

'I see. You mean a kind of Commoners' Party? A party for the man in the street?'

'Yeah, that's the idea.'

'Inkerman Street, where they all wear slippers.' This was from Simon Speirs.

'I beg your pardon, Simon?'

'Oh, nothing, Mrs Baxter,' he drawled.

She returned to Baz. 'Go on, dear, about your campaign.'

'Well, that's it, really, it's a sort of "people's party", but for the school. You see,' he went on, getting bolder, in spite of Speirs and Co., 'this school's OK, but I feel it's too – too –'

'Too much for the élite, dear?'

Baz looked slightly embarrassed. He didn't really know what 'élite' meant. He'd always been going to look it up.

'That means too much concentration on the people who've, well, you know, got a lot of privileges already, giving them even more,' she said helpfully. 'Is that what you mean?'

'Yes, I suppose so. I just want things to be a bit fairer. That's all.'

Granny B. was flicking through rows of cassette boxes. 'The People's Party . . .' she muttered, '. . . the Common People . . . the Common *Man*. Ah, yes, here we go,' and she pulled out a tape.

'I'll do it, Mrs Baxter.' Jake was already at her elbow, reformed, apart from his hopeless orange mop.

'*No, thank you*, Peter.'

'Jake, actually. Go on, I'll put it on for you.'

'I can manage myself, thank you.'

Seconds later, the most amazing sound Baz had ever heard filled the music room. It was marvellous, all brass and great booming drums, a glorious golden fanfare, that made you think you were seventeen feet tall, and striding among mountains, king of the world. It was the sort of music that set your blood pounding, the sort that, when it was over, which was much, much too soon for Baz, made you want to cry. He did cry too, a bit, and to hide his face he had to lift the desk lid, though it wasn't his desk, or his class-room, pretending to scrabble inside. This was the kind of music they should have played for his father when they'd said goodbye to him at that hideous crematorium. They'd needed comfort then, and this music was comforting. But it was mighty also. It was music for the best people, the best people in the world.

But it only lasted for a few minutes. Granny Baxter clicked off the tape recorder and there was absolute silence in the class-room. 'Well, dear,' she said to Baz at last, 'what did you think of that? Come on, put your desk lid down now. I played it especially for you, you know, don't play silly games.'

Even now Baz could hardly speak, 'I'm not, miss, only, listen, that's *fantastic*, it's just, oh, I don't know ... It'd be great for my election campaign, it'd be fabulous. It's real ... victory music, isn't it?' And his face was shining.

Obviously gratified, Granny Baxter took the tape from the machine, put it in its box and gave it to him. 'Here, you can borrow it, dear, listen to it at home and if you really do want to use it we will see if we can make you a copy. Better still, a few of you could get together and play it yourselves. Here you are.'

Baz's fingers trembled as he took the box from her and glanced at the label. It said, *Aaron Copland: Fanfare for the Common Man*. He'd like to meet this Mr Copland. He'd tell *him* about Dad.

9

On the following Monday, Slime made a surprise announcement in Prayers about the election. 'You've had several weeks to sort your ideas out,' he said, the keen hawk face which Baz didn't quite trust shining with enthusiasm and *bonhomie*, 'and I sense that the general excitement is mounting, which is jolly good. Now, though, it's time to go *public*. I want election papers in tomorrow, please, for those who have decided to run, and on Friday this assembly will be extended so that all candidates can have a chance to put their case – *briefly*, I should add. All details will be posted up on a special election notice-board in General Area A. So, get down to your speech-making, all you budding politicians, and, er, jolly good luck.'

There was a fair buzz of excitement as the school trailed out of the Anderson Hall, the new auditorium which had been built last year with money donated by Sir Albert, who'd more recently put up the cash for the new tennis-courts. 'Why does he always talk to us as if we've got a mental age of three?' growled Polly in Baz's ear. 'Jolly this, jolly that, honestly, how *old* does he think we are?'

'*No talking!*' snapped Jugsy, who was on duty at the door. He was looking rather more grim than usual, and Baz had seen him shaking his head lugubriously when Slime made the announcement about Friday's assembly, and sorrowfully wringing his hands. Polly had heard that he was dead against the school election, that he believed it would cause 'rowdyism' and wild behaviour, that it was generally Bad News.

They didn't know this from Jugsy himself, in public he was absolutely loyal to Slime, whatever he might think privately. No, they got it from Polly's friend, Matt Pearson, the boy in

3M who was helping him run his Green campaign. Matt had fallen arches and couldn't do sport this term, so he helped Keith Slack with odd jobs round the PE department. On match days he was allowed to stand and watch on the field. And it was on one of these occasions that he'd listened in on a conversation between Jugsy and Slime. You couldn't call it 'eavesdropping', Slime had a very thin and penetrating voice (it matched his nose), and Matt had very sharp ears (they made up for his flat feet).

What he heard was very interesting because it wasn't just the headmaster's views on his great election idea, but his views on Baz as well. He was very proud of him, according to Matt, said he was Bryce's best scholarship winner for years and that his great sporting talents were 'jam on the bread' or something. But Jugsy had been extremely cautious, said that somebody like Baz Bradshaw needed 'the talent to *handle* his talent' and that he wasn't sure the boy had it. 'The mother does little cleaning jobs I gather,' he added distastefully. 'That won't help his image when he runs in this election of yours. It's not exactly glamorous.'

Baz was speechless when he heard this particular piece of snobbery from Matt. He wanted to go to Jugsy straight away and tell him that your home background meant absolutely nothing, that it was what you *were*, the kind of person, that mattered. Anyhow, he was proud of the way his mother had gone and fixed up all those jobs, after Dad. She did the early morning office cleaning twice a week, but she was a home help mainly, to old ladies, doing their cleaning and shopping. Sometimes she helped them have baths and go to the toilet. It was rotten when you were old, she said. *That* was real life, what *she* saw, not the kind of life Jugsy lived at Bryce's, hidden from the facts inside his academic gown. He was supposed to have done things in the Second World War, but you couldn't believe *that*. Someone should tackle him about his snobbish remarks, but of course Baz couldn't. He wasn't supposed to know.

Apparently, Slime hadn't been very interested in Jugsy's views on Baz's mother anyhow. He was much more interested in whether Bryce's were going to win this hockey match against Eave's Hall School, and Baz had scored two goals in rapid succession. 'Jolly, jolly good!' he chortled, in that irritating way of his, while Jugsy trotted after him along the touchline, trying to explain his worries about the new boy. Matt hadn't been able to hear all of it, he edged up a bit too close he said and got suspicious looks from Jugsy. But he did hear the main worry, which was simply that Baz was getting rather popular in the middle school, gathering something he called a little 'coterie' around him, to explain what Jugsy had rudely referred to as his 'tinpot' views. 'He may *win* your election,' he said. 'Think of that, this common man nonsense, all over Bryce's.'

'Oh, I don't think so, flash-in-the-pan stuff, Henry – oh, *bad luck*, school!' as Dogger Benson in goal let a ball through, evening up the score.

Baz told The Cow about what Matt had overheard at the match. His face was completely healed up now, with no scar, so it wouldn't prevent him going in for beauty competitions, she told him with a smile. But he'd taken to dropping in on her now and again, during the long lunch-break, if he wasn't needed for anything. He rather liked sitting with the fat, lazy cat on his knee and having a mug of tea with her. She didn't seem to mind his visits, as long as she didn't have anyone's cuts and bruises to see to, of course.

She seemed a bit sceptical about what he'd heard from Matt Pearson. 'I'd take that with a large pinch of salt, if I were you, Baz,' she said, handing him tea in his favourite 'I love Liverpool' mug. 'Don't forget that Matt is running for the Green Party with your friend Polly. I mean, he could be making it all up, just to put you off your stroke.'

'Ne'er,' Baz said stoutly. 'Matt's not like that. Anyhow, they're trying to get me to join up with them. And Jugsy *is* a snob. He's always going on about the "image" of Bryce's. *Image*, it's all he cares about.'

'I like him,' The Cow said, unexpectedly.

He stared at her. '*Why*?' Like that dried-up old stick, how could she? Whose side was she on?

'Well, I know he's got his little ways, but, oh, I dunno, he's so loyal to this place, Baz. He's had military training you know, that's one reason everything has to be *just right*. This school is his whole life now.'

'That's what Vanessa says. I think it's a bit pathetic.'

'How's it going then, your love-life?' She clearly didn't want to discuss Mr Moncrieff any more.

Baz blushed, 'There isn't one. Her mother's very strict. She's always waiting in their front room at half-past four, to make sure she comes straight home from the bus. And she's not allowed out in the evenings because of homework and her music practice. She does ballet too.'

'What about the weekends?'

'Oh, we've not got round to weekends,' he said gloomily. The truth was he was still much too shy to go round to her house, or to ask her out. He'd have to get the money off his mother and there'd be a lot of heavy questions, then. He'd thought of asking her round one Saturday, to watch a video, but when he saw the house she lived in, his courage failed. It was one of those mansion-type places in Denning. Her father must make a real bomb from the Orlando boutiques: one in Darnley, one in Wilmslow and one in Cheadle. Then he brightened. 'She's coming to my election planning meeting this week, anyhow. The only snag is, it's got to be in Alice Sugden's garage. We need room to spread out, you see, to make the posters and stuff.'

'Doesn't Alice approve of Vanessa?'

'Oh, yeah, yes she does. They've made friends and everything, only . . . I think she's you know . . .' he wriggled.

'A bit jealous?'

'Yeah. Well, we've been friends since the juniors, only I don't, you know . . .'

'Fancy her?'

'Well, no.'

'Mrs Baxter tells me she's fixed you up with some election music.'

'Yeah,' Baz beamed and hummed the beginning. 'It's called "Fanfare for the Common Man". It's fantastic. We'll probably end up playing the tape on Friday, when I make my first public speech, but she's written it out for us and made it a bit simpler, and we are going to see if we can play it ourselves, like. Jake Elder's a fantastic drummer and Alice says he can play their Antony's drums, he's got them all set up in the garage. Vanessa's learnt the horn part and Alice is playing the trumpet. That's the bit I'm worried about actually.'

'Why?'

'Well, she's not really very *good*.' The truth was, Alice on the trumpet sounded like a constipated duck, but you couldn't tell *her* that. She was so anxious to have live music for Friday morning, and her mother had fixed up for them to use the garage and borrow their Antony's drums. It was all because she wanted Alice to shine of course. He ought to be sympathetic about that side of it, at least.

'Oh, well,' The Cow said easily, draining off her tea. 'No doubt you will sort it out. I rather like the sound of these loony people. I think I'll vote for Harriet Weatherall. I'm fond of jelly.'

'What about *us*?' Baz said indignantly. 'You can't waste your vote. We're a *serious* party.'

The Cow laughed. 'Don't worry, the staff don't get a vote. It's strictly "school only".'

'Would you vote for me, if you did have one?'

She hesitated. 'Not sure, Baz, to be honest. You're campaigning for the ordinary person aren't you, and although I *believe* in the ordinary person, I honestly think it all sounds a bit dull.'

'Oh.' Baz was quite offended. He thought The Cow was his secret champion, that she'd have been certain to cast her vote his way.

'Have I said the wrong thing?' she muttered, when she saw his face.

'Well, no . . .' he said slowly. 'But it's *not* dull, my party, honestly. The point is, people should start off with the same chances in a place like this. I don't mean you've got to stay ordinary for ever and ever, of course not. I mean, look at Sir Albert Anderson. He's a millionaire now, and he came from the back streets of Darnley.'

'*Baz*,' she said reproachfully, 'surely you don't want to hold *him* up as an example for people to copy? Honestly, that man, he's a real toad. He's always coming round here to check up on what's happening to his precious money, his "brass" as he calls it; he's power-crazed. He doesn't trust the head either, he's an awful little man. You don't want people to end up like *him*, do you?'

'No, no of course not. I'm just saying . . . background doesn't matter. The way you speak doesn't matter either. But listen, Cut Above are campaigning for elocution lessons, it's in their manifesto. Can you believe that?'

The Cow looked embarrassed, then she said, 'I agree that accent doesn't matter, so long as people speak reasonably correctly, in a way that makes them understood, but I —'

'But what about uniform?' Baz broke in heatedly. 'Think of all the time you have to waste, checking up on whether people are dressed properly. It's just a waste of time, the teachers don't wear uniform.'

'I do.'

'Yes, but that's only because of your job. What I am trying to say, and what I'll say on Friday, is that that side of this place is so . . . *petty*. It's not about that is it?'

'What's not?'

'Well, *Life*.'

'Ah, yes. Good old Life,' she said mysteriously. 'Listen, lovey – oh, you have to go, that's the bell – just take *care*, will you? Promise The Cow.'

'What do you mean "take care"?'

'Well, you're very *new*, lovey. I know you've made some friends but you've got a few enemies, too. I hear about these things.'

'Huh, don't tell *me*.'

'And Mr Moncrieff's got a point you know, worrying that things might get out of hand with this election. You must have heard about the fence.'

'Do you mean "Bryce's stinks"? That's nothing, honestly, you should see *our* school buildings, I mean the place I used to go to, with Alice. You should see those for graffiti.'

'But it wasn't just what they painted on the fence, Baz. They threw bricks at it too, they caused a lot of damage. If anyone had been around they could have been hurt, Baz.'

'What are you telling me this for?' he said hotly. 'Do you think it was something to do with me?'

She hesitated.

'You *do*, don't you?' he accused, tipping the cat off his knee and rising with some difficulty from the saggy old chair.

'*Calm down*, pet. Of course it's nothing to do with you. But I did hear in the staff-room that the head had been on to the Comprehensive about the fence, that they'd questioned some of the boys in the third year, and that, well your name cropped up.'

Kev, Kev White and possibly Alex Brodey. He tightened his mouth just in case she asked him anything. How *could* they? They were asking for trouble, they were crazy, to make attacks on Bryce's.

'Off you go,' she said kindly. 'I'm sorry if I've said all the wrong things, Baz, but I'm only trying to help. People will be watching you very closely during this election thing, they will be waiting for you to put a foot wrong, and then, "bingo". You see, in a place like this you've got to *earn* the right to change things, Baz. It's all been here a very long time, going along in its sweet, old-fashioned way.'

'*Sweet*?' growled Baz. 'Huh.'

'So "make haste slowly", Mr Bradshaw, that's my advice,' she said, opening the door for him.

'*Festina lente*, that's the Latin for it,' he told her proudly, '*Hurry slowly*, we've been doing Latin tags, with Jugsy.'

'Oh, stop showing off,' and she gave him a friendly shove through the door.

Mum was right, he thought, as he walked down the corridor. He never could resist the chance to shine.

10

Alice Sugden's peculiarly loud and penetrating voice was continuing to drive Baz mad, but Kev and Alex were grateful for it. They wanted to know what was happening in his stupid 'Common Man' campaign, and it was Alice who yelled out the arrangements for Tuesday night, at the bottom of Inkerman Street.

'*What's* your number, Alice?' This was Jake Elder, who was obviously going to muscle in on their big election meeting in the garage. He had not actually *said* he was voting for Baz yet, but he'd offered to play the drums for them, if they wanted. Drummers were rather thin on the ground, he'd told them. They'd be wise to accept. Baz was doubtful. He sensed that Jake Elder wasn't altogether reliable. But they couldn't find anyone else, so he said he could come, as an 'observer'.

'Seventy Two. It's semi-detached with bay windows. Come at 5.30, oh, and Mummy says all shoes to be left at the door because of the new carpet squares.'

When the Baz group had dispersed, Kev and Alex slid round the corner into Inkerman Street. Alex was grinning broadly. '5.30 at number Seventy Two. So now we know. Why don't we pay them a little visit?'

'What for?' Kev was growing more and more suspicious of Alex. He'd not much liked being put through the third degree at school by Mr Greaves, about what had been done to Bryce's fence. True he'd been there at the time, but he'd not done the spraying, and he'd not heaved those bricks through either, the week after. That had been Alex as well. He didn't really understand the way his mind worked. After all, it wasn't *Alex's* Dad who was out of work because the Pullen's Field building project had been scrapped, and the new snooty Baz Bradshaw hadn't been *Alex*'s friend. But he'd got this thing about Bryce's now, and about Baz; somehow he'd taken up the cause for the rejected Kev White, or so he said. But Kev didn't quite trust his motives. He was just restless and bored, he just wanted to make trouble, *any* kind of trouble, to liven things up. Of course, he'd lied his head off about Bryce's fence, and Mr Greaves had had to put the whole thing 'on ice'. But he said he was keeping his eye on 'certain people in the middle school', from now on.

Kev reminded Alex of this now. 'Listen, don't let's make any trouble,' he said rather nervously. You had to be careful with Alex Brodey, he had a very nasty tongue. He could be as nice as pie with you one minute, and foul the next. Kev didn't have a special friend to go round with now Baz had gone to Bryce's, so he didn't want Alex to turn on him. But he was fearful of what he might be planning to do next. His dad would hit him, if he got into trouble at school, and if he'd been drinking and went for him ... it didn't bear thinking about.

'You chickening out or something?' Alex said sourly.

'Chickening out of what?'

'Well, us and Bryce's.'

'No, course not.' But he wanted to, deep down. He thought it was stupid. What could they achieve with bricks and aerosols? It was what Bryce's stood for that got him, which was why he'd gone along with Alex at first. And yet, part of him still wanted to *be* there with Baz. Of course he was angry about the tennis-courts; he thought it was plain greedy, having those, and it had put his father out of a job. But, though he'd never admit it to anyone, he'd quite like to have been going to a place like that, with all its fantastic equipment, its marvellous buildings, its extra lessons for this and that. And, if Baz was telling the truth, he wanted the same as Kev wanted, which was for *everyone* to have equal chances. That was part of the essay he'd written, the one he and Alex had scribbled over on the bus. Sometimes, now, he rather wanted to talk to Baz. He didn't look very happy these days, and his dad had heard – from someone else's dad in the Bay Horse, a man with kids at Bryce's – that Baz Bradshaw didn't seem to have any friends much, even though he was doing so brilliantly.

He muttered, 'I don't think we should wreck their meeting, Alex. Alice'd go straight to her mother, and she'd make big trouble. She's that sort.'

'I didn't say anything about wrecking it, did I? No, I think we should, y'know, just hang about a bit, just see what they're planning next. Could be useful.'

'You mean, listen in?'

'If we can. If it's like our garage, there'll be a window in the back. It sounds posh. *Carpet squares*! Anyhow, meet you here at 5.30. OK?'

'OK,' Kev said, uncertainly.

Alex's weaselly face suddenly narrowed. 'You are coming, aren't you? It's only a bit of fun.'

'Of course I'm coming.' But Kev felt sick at heart. Alex's last 'fun' had led to that extremely difficult interview with Mr Greaves. Perhaps he should have told the headmaster the truth. At least it would have got Alex off his back.

The Sugdens' was the poshest garage Baz had ever been in. It wasn't used for the car, there was a carport in the front of the house for that. It was really a games room with a table-tennis set and a dartboard, and radiators to keep everything warm and dry. It was so hot Alice opened the window when everyone had arrived. That was extremely useful for Kev and Alex, who, in the dusk, had taken up their positions outside, in the narrow strip of garden between the garage wall and the back fence.

'Shoes off, everyone!' shrilled Alice. 'These carpet tiles are new you see. Shoes on the mat please.'

Baz unlaced his sneakers gloomily, with some misgiving. Because they were on Alice's territory she was being rather bossier than usual. He wanted the meeting to go well, but this wasn't a very promising start. And what if she was funny about Vanessa? She could well be, because of all the stuff she'd brought from Orlando, not to mention her superiority on the French horn.

Everyone was supposed to help do designs on the T-shirts and badges first, and to paint posters, but Jake was already totally absorbed in Antony Sugden's drum-kit. He'd got Granny Baxter's tape of 'Fanfare for the Common Man' going on a Walkman and he kept doing great deafening drum-rolls. 'Be careful!' warned Alice. 'You might split the skins. Our Antony'll go mad if those get damaged.'

'Alice,' Jake pointed out, 'they're *drums*, or haven't you noticed? You're *meant* to make a noise with them.'

'Yes, but our Antony, you know . . .'

Jake drummed on, oblivious, a far-away smile on his lips while the others helped Alice spread newspapers on the table-tennis top, so they could get to work.

From one of the factories that supplied his shops, Mr Honeywell had got a whole box of plain white T-shirts. They'd collected some money between them and bought a kit to decorate them, and Alice had brought a box of old lapel badges. 'It's our Antony's collection,' she said. 'He doesn't want them now he's at university, so he's let me have them. Look I've stuck white paper on them all, so we can just colour over it. We can give them out to people.'

Baz was impressed. There must have been at least fifty badges in the old tin and re-covering them so neatly must have taken Alice hours and hours. 'You're brilliant,' he said, running his hands through them.

'Thanks, Baz.' And she snuggled up to him. He realized at once that he'd make a tactical error. It was fatal to give her any encouragement whatever. Why couldn't she get the message about Vanessa?

Jake had done a design for Baz's Common Man Party, even though, so far, he'd not *officially* joined their campaign. He still reckoned he was a 'floating voter'. The design was very simple, a big yellow trumpet, slanting from top to bottom, and coming out of the business end the words 'Vote for Baz' in capitals, with a few music notes drifting about. 'That's all you need,' he said proudly, climbing out from behind the drum-kit. 'I'll sketch it in for you on the T-shirts and posters, then you can do the colouring in.' He examined the T-shirt kit Baz had bought. 'Hmm, this'll be fine so long as you don't *wash* them.'

Alice looked alarmed. 'But Mummy'll insist,' she said plaintively. 'She washes everything, even when it's not dirty.'

'Well, you'll just have to hide it from her, then,' said Jake. 'Anyhow, you'll only be allowed to wear it on Slime's campaign days. It's not exactly going to get sweaty, Alice.'

The fat girl blushed. 'No, all right. I can always put it in my shoe-bag. She won't look in there. Oh, but it'll get all creased then . . .'

'Alice,' Baz said firmly, 'it doesn't *matter*. Now do you think you could transfer Jake's trumpet design to the badges, then I'll start colouring them in.'

While they worked, they listened to 'Fanfare for the Common Man' on Vanessa's ghetto blaster to get them into the right mood. The amazing music filled the concrete garage and a kind of stillness settled down on them all as they drew and painted and glued. Baz knew every note of the piece now, he'd been listening to it at home on Dad's cassette player. But he still couldn't get to the end without his eyes filling up with tears. It was such marvellous music, the kind that made you feel that nothing bad could ever happen again, that it *was* worth going on with things for him and Mum, even without his father around. Somehow Dad was there, *in* the music.

But their attempts to play it live brought a sudden embarrassing end to these great dreams of his. When the posters and T-shirts were finished and they'd all taken a few badges to finish off at home, Alice set up the music stands she'd borrowed from her mother and organized the three instrumentalists. Granny Baxter had come up trumps and three copies of a simplified version of the music now lay open ready. Baz couldn't wait. They'd all been practising at home, and he could just imagine people's surprise in Friday's assembly when instead of a tinny tape, real live music came pouring forth from three live musicians.

Jake started it with some magnificent drum-rolls. So far it sounded pretty good, though obviously not nearly as professional as the tape, not yet. But the point was that it was *live*. Then Alice put her trumpet to her lips and blew. That did it. She was OK for a few minutes, quite good, in fact, then the most awful squeaking noises started coming out; Jake and Vanessa immediately stopped playing and looked at her in dismay. 'I'm sorry,' she said, turning pink, 'but even the simplified version is difficult, Mr Gordon said. So can we start again?'

'OK, sure,' Jake muttered, but he looked very doubtful as he picked up his drum sticks. Vanessa looked plain embarrassed and slightly irritated too, Baz thought. She'd been going through her part every lunch-time, in the practice rooms at school. He'd hung about, hoping they could talk.

This time Alice sounded even worse. She couldn't get the higher notes at all. Her face bulged scarlet and her eyes popped. Jake snorted, abandoned the drums, picked up a comic from a stack of old newspapers and started to read it, pointedly. Vanessa said timidly, 'Should we have another go, Alice?' But *someone* had laughed, and the fat girl suddenly burst into tears. 'Listen, mine's the hardest part,' she spluttered. 'I've only just done Grade Three you know. Why don't *you* have a go, Basil Bradshaw, instead of just standing there, laughing at me. Go on, *you* have a try.'

Baz, frightened the trumpet might get dropped and bring down the wrath of Mother Sugden upon them, took it from her, but he was bewildered. 'I *didn't* laugh, honestly.' Alice was usually quite tough. It wasn't like her to burst into tears.

'You *did*,' she sniffed. 'I heard you.'

'Alice, you're imagining things. Listen, we'll use the tape on

101

Friday. If we can get the proper music together for The Day then we will but, honestly, it doesn't matter.'

'YOU LAUGHED AT ME, BAZ BRADSHAW.'

'I DIDN'T.'

There was an awful silence in the garage. Outside, under the window, Alex and Kev didn't dare move a muscle. *They'd* laughed, because it had sounded so very funny. Fat Alice's attempts to play Bradshaw's election masterpiece had been just like a cow in pain.

'My mother said we could make tea if we wanted,' she told them. 'She's put a kettle out and things. No, *I'll* do it, that's all I'm fit for, obviously, brewing tea and providing garages for people. You get on with your meeting, don't mind me.' She was still crying a bit, but it had reached the sniffy stage now.

Baz put his arm round her. 'Listen, I'm sorry, Alice. Nobody meant to laugh.' (Who had, anyhow? *He'd* not.) 'I had no idea it was so hard, honestly. The garage is really great and we are really grateful to your Mum and your Antony, and especially now you've got carpet tiles . . .' he floundered helplessly.

'Come on, Allie,' Vanessa said, hugging her on the other side. 'We've got a lot to get through and my father's picking me up at 7.30. I've got a music lesson. Come *on* . . . Who cares about doing the silly old music live, anyhow?'

She did though, otherwise she surely wouldn't have done all that extra practising at school. Baz watched her, delicately sipping her tea, one arm still firmly round Alice, and his love grew.

For the business part of the meeting, he produced a clipboard and made notes. The first thing was to settle Jake's position. 'Are you voting for me or not?' he challenged him. 'Because if you're not, I think you ought to leave at this point. This part of the meeting is private.'

Jake, making soft feathery sounds on the drum, with special brushes, looked injured. 'Listen, mate. I've designed your logo haven't I, and I've played these drums for you, not that we've got very far.'

'Yes, well, we won't go into that. Are you voting for me? Last I heard, you were supporting the Cliff Richard lot.'

'Oh, *them*. Ne'er, they're turning out to be a bit pathetic, I think. I mean, it rained on their first proper playground meeting and they all ran inside, *and* they let Jugsy confiscate 'Congratulations'. No, I've gone off them. Really, up to now, I've been a floating voter.'

'OK, you can float off, then,' said Baz.

But Jake was still brushing the drums lovingly. 'No, I'll come in with you Baz, honestly, I *will*. But I seriously think you should accept Polly's offer and join up with the Greens. He's quite popular, you know. You'd win, between you.'

'Oh, I'm not sure,' Baz said doubtfully. There was nothing in Polly's Green manifesto that he didn't agree with, in fact, he felt rather bad about never really having thought about 'Green' problems before, but . . . *joining up*: he'd got his Common Man Party now and he wanted to lead it into victory. He *must* be the leader. His mother was right about him, he did like glory. But there had to *be* leaders in everything. 'What does anyone else think?' he said.

'I think you should join Polly,' Vanessa said firmly.

'So do I.' Alice was rather better-tempered now. She was on to her fifth chocolate digestive biscuit, Baz had been counting. That used up nearly half her calories for the day, he reckoned. Mum dieted too, so he knew. What had happened to the 'Thin is Beautiful' regime?

'The problem with going in with Polly and the Greens is Pullen's Field,' he said. 'Polly wants to leave it wild for the birds and stuff, you know, a sort of nature reserve. But I still think they should build those houses on it. Firstly, people have got to live somewhere, and secondly a lot of people are out of a job because the scheme has been scrapped. My friend Kev's dad's one of them. It's terrible for him, he was relying on that work.'

In the damp darkness behind the garage, Kev's cheeks burned, and an unexpected lump came into his throat. He was glad Alex Brodey was hearing this, and glad that Baz hadn't dumped him as a friend. He couldn't have blamed him if he had, the way he had treated him lately. He rather wanted to shake Alex off and try to make it up between them. But how? Alex had this hold over people. Once he'd labelled you 'his mate' that was it. He wasn't so easy to get rid of.

Jake said, 'I think you and Polly could work the Pullen's Field thing out, Baz. Polly's not going to concentrate just on that, it'd lose him too many votes from the sports fanatics. Votes are the thing, mate, and people know Polly. He's dead popular too. Now, they don't really know you yet, and I reckon you need him more than he needs you.'

'I'd want to lead the party,' Baz said stolidly. 'You've got to have a figure-head in a election, and I think . . . Well, I think it should be me, that's all. In fact, *Polly* said it ought to be me. No, I'm still not sure . . .'

'Tell you another thing . . .' Jake muttered, ignoring the bit about the figure-head, which, as it left Baz's lips, he instantly regretted, it had sounded so pushy. (Why hadn't he kept his big mouth shut?) 'Tell you another thing, Polly's dad works for Pennine TV. He's Jack Pollitt. He does all their outside broadcasts. You could get on the box. *Everyone*'d see you then. Millions of people watch telly.'

Having felt doubtful about the Bradshaw–Pollitt merger, Baz immediately perked up. 'TV. Do you really think so? That would be fantastic.' He could already see it, Baz Bradshaw, of Bryce's Common Man Party, talking to a roving reporter somewhere in Darnley, the music of 'Fanfare' subtly playing in the background as the cameras rolled, Slime agog in front of his television set.

He said thoughtfully, 'OK, I'll think about going in with Polly. Come on, we'd better clear up, it's nearly half-past seven.'

'I'd *definitely* think about it, you'd be silly not to,' Jake said softly, an enigmatic smile playing round his mouth. He'd known the mention of TV would do the trick. He'd got Baz Bradshaw well and truly sussed out.

*

Kev felt a bit crushed as he walked down Inkerman Street with Alex Brodey, disappointed, and confused. What did Baz *really* think about anything, and was he only interested in promoting himself, in the end? He had argued for keeping the building scheme, but *why*, that was the point? Was he like all the grown up people in politics, just saying what suited him best at the time? That's what his father reckoned politicians were like, anyhow. He didn't trust any of them.

Alex was in no doubt at all about Baz's motives. 'He'll join Polly,' he said. 'He doesn't give a damn about Green issues, if you ask me, he just wants the votes. He's got a head as big as a bus, too. Did you notice how quickly he changed his mind, when he thought he might go on television? He's just an attention-grabber. But if he *does* go Green, mate, we can't let it rest, can we? I mean, that really does put the tin lid on your father's job, doesn't it?'

'How?'

'Well, he'd be supporting the party that wants to keep Pullen's Field as it is, of course. Don't be so thick.'

'Don't see what we can do about it,' Kev said gloomily. He was cold, stiff and hungry from crouching down behind that garage for so long, and he wanted to go home.

'We can do a lot, mate. He disgusts me, your fine friend, Bradshaw. Oh, yes. We can do a lot, y'know, make life a bit less pleasant for him, and for that school. It disgusts me. He disgusts me.'

Kev managed to get away, trying to convince himself that Alex Brodey was all talk. But there had been the graffiti and the bricks, and now, obviously, he was planning something bigger. 'Mega' had been the word he'd used, as he went off. If only Kev could get away from him. But that wasn't going to be easy. He felt trapped.

11
***

Granny Baxter wasn't the most brilliant music teacher in the world, but she was extremely useful, because she was such an old gossip; also you could side-track her very easily in lessons, and that's exactly what Baz and Polly did, the day before they made their speeches.

Polly and his friend Matt Pearson had spent the whole week doing a poll, going round at dinner times to find out how people intended to vote, and they'd been allowed to analyse their findings on the school computer. So far it seemed that Cut Above and Polly's Greens were neck and neck, with Baz and Common Man a little way behind. Harriet's Jelly Party was doing pretty well too, for a loony; it was only Clifford Turner who was really trailing. He blamed it all on Jugsy, for taking away 'Congratulations'. He was losing heart because people were drifting away and joining other parties. Julius Malin had done a poll too, and he claimed that Polly's figures were rubbish. Cut Above was way in front according to him, and nobody else in with a chance. Baz received this news gloomily. He'd been very surprised to hear that he was running behind Polly. Common Man was all over the school with its bright-yellow posters and its trumpet badges. Everyone was talking about it, and people were still turning up in droves to listen to his campaign speeches, there seemed to be more than ever. He definitely attracted more interest than anyone else. Polly, still anxious to get Baz to join up with him, was generously reassuring. 'Surely you don't imagine that Malin's telling the truth about his poll, do you?' he said. 'You can fix figures you know. It depresses the other parties, it puts them off their stroke. The point about an election campaign is that it's, well, sort of psychological warfare.'

'Perhaps you fixed your figures, too, then?' Baz suggested suspiciously.

'No, I've not, honestly. As far as I can see, the general picture is the one I have given you. Now, if you joined up with us, "Go Green with Baz", or something, we'd honestly win, hands down.'

But Baz still couldn't quite bring himself to go in with Polly. The latest was that Kev White's father had been picked up drunk and disorderly on their street a couple of nights ago, and he'd had to go to the police station. Baz felt really sorry for him, and for Kev. That sort of behaviour had *got* to be something to do with losing his job at Ridgeways. He'd been OK before, even when his wife walked out. As far as the election was concerned the big problem was Pullen's Field. How could he join a campaign that was against building those houses? If they *were* to join up, one of them would have to give way.

The staff, or what Slime pretentiously called the 'Senior Common Room', didn't have a vote in the election. It was 'school only'. But according to Granny Baxter the teachers had definite views on the campaign. They'd had a special meeting about it, and Jugsy had really let rip apparently, to Slime.

'He's worried, dears,' she told them in their Thursday afternoon music lesson. 'He still thinks things are going to get out of control. Oh, the poor man does *fret* so. I've told him before, it's very bad for his blood pressure, but of course he won't listen to me, he thinks I'm just a silly old woman, I suppose. But you *do* have to watch it, and he's at a funny age.'

'Mrs Baxter,' interrupted Baz, not wanting her to get launched into the story of Mr Moncrieff's mid-life crisis, '*why* is he so worried? I mean, it's only a bit of fun, this election lark.' Though he didn't mean that it was a 'lark' for a minute and everyone in the room knew it. Baz Bradshaw was all out to win; it was written all over him.

'Well, you know we've had vandals, dear, slogans painted on the fences, and people throwing bricks about.'

'But that was nothing to *do* with the election, Mrs Baxter,' Baz protested.

'Pull the other one, Bradshaw, it's got bells on,' Simon Speirs muttered behind his hand. 'We all know who is responsible. We didn't have any problems here before *you* joined the school.'

Granny B., not hearing Speirs's *sotto voce* drawl, carried on.

'Maybe not, dear, but it's the *tone* of things that Mr Moncrieff doesn't like, and, I'm sorry to say, he did complain again about your ear-rings. *Do* take them out, dear. You know it's against the school rules and so *bad* for you. They could cause an infection, and then where would you be?'

Baz removed the small gold ear-rings instantly. He always did when the teachers asked him to, but not without trying to engage them on the general subject of uniform. He wore them for his meetings on principle, it was part of his campaign, part of his view that life held more important issues than regulation shoes and shirts, and regulation ears. People like Jugsy seemed to devote all their energies to the petty things, to the things that didn't matter. Tomorrow, in assembly, he was going to tell them what did. He said, 'What do the other teachers think about the election, then?'

'Oh, we all think it's rather wonderful, dear. It's livened things up no end. As Mr Lyme says, it's brought out people's creative sides, it's made them think for themselves. He thinks it's marvellous, how you and your friends are going to play the Copland tomorrow.'

Baz, Alice and Vanessa exchanged helpless looks at this point. They'd not been able to bring themselves to confess that they had scrapped their live performance. She was so proud of them. 'Mr Slack's all for it, too,' she went on, 'and Matron, *and* me. Of course, there are one or two who are rather less keen, I have to admit.'

'Who?' Baz asked.

'Well, I can't go telling tales out of school dear, but Dr Prout feels rather the same as Mr Moncrieff, I think, and Mr

Banerjee has no time for it either, I'm afraid. But generally, I'd say we are more *in* favour than *not*. And, personally, I'm greatly looking forward to tomorrow morning.'

Baz wasn't. When he allowed himself to think about it, his insides turned to water. He'd written and rewritten his speech till he knew it upside-down and back to front, and he'd got notes, typed out on Dad's old portable. The funny thing was that when the moment arrived for him to deliver it, it came out quite differently, *and it didn't matter*.

There they all were, on the platform, lined up next to Slime, and people were laughing their heads off. It was no wonder, Harriet Weatherall looked so fantastic, completely enclosed in a wobbling jelly costume, made of foam and cardboard. She had to be helped up the steps to take her place, the peep-holes that she'd made for her eyes weren't quite big enough. Baz looked at her costume with genuine admiration. It was home-made and it was absolutely brilliant, all fluted and bobbled, just like a giant jelly out of a book of fairy-tales, and she had a big foam cherry tied on top of her head for a hat. Next to Harriet stood Polly, and Baz had to admit that he was second best, the original 'Green Man' – Dad had read him a story called that once, about a giant. Both Polly and Harriet had this fairy-tale feel though, it was uncanny. Perhaps, it'd mean that nobody was going to take them very seriously, he thought, rather selfishly.

Polly's basic outfit was simple, a green T-shirt and green camouflage trousers from the Army Surplus Store in town, but he was wearing bright-green make-up and he'd powdered his hair with something green too. He'd back-combed it so that it stuck out all over in little tufts, and into the tufts he stuck bits of twig. He even had a little stuffed bird sitting on it. Next to him stood Julius Malin and frankly he looked plain boring, just his usual neat self, except that he was even more clean and more combed than usual; so sparkling bright in fact, from the top of his glossy blond head to the tips of his black mirror shoes, that he looked as if he'd been through a human car-wash, then through a valeting service. Baz inspected his uniform. It was perfect. If it wasn't brand-new for the occasion, then it certainly had been given the Golden Dollar treatment, that thing that cost you extra at the dry cleaners. He carried a great sheaf of notes.

Baz felt reassured when he saw those. Thank goodness that something about him was less than perfect. Slime had said that each speaker could only have three minutes, but Malin had enough notes with him to last into next week. Baz's were typed on postcards which he'd stuck in the top pocket of his denim jacket. He'd have liked to glance at them while they were singing the hymn, just to refresh his memory, but he daren't. You were so exposed up here, he was glad he'd not put on anything too outrageous. Apart from his ear-rings (great clanging brass ones, borrowed from Mum) he looked pretty much as usual, just 'pre-Bryce's', in fact, neat, but not too neat, in his denim jacket and his jeans and the button-down blue shirt that Simon Speirs had ripped. Underneath he was wearing one of the new trumpet T-shirts, but the design was carefully hidden for now; its moment would come later.

Clifford Turner looked like Clifford Turner, but deeply dejected. He was wearing a campaign T-shirt too. It had a big grinning Cliff Richard on it and the slogan 'We're all going on a summer holiday'. Apart from that he'd made no effort at all. Apparently he was very nervous about having to speak in the hall, said he'd give up, scrap his party, hardly anyone would vote for it anyhow. But his form teacher, Mr Banerjee, had said very sternly that he had 'put his hand to the plough', or something, and that he owed it to his supporters to go through with it now. *Poor Cliff.* Baz felt a bit sorry for him, and embarrassed too, because most of the original supporters had come over to his side.

Slime asked Harriet to kick off, because she was a girl. Someone in the hall hissed 'sexist' and someone else shouted 'take a vote on it'. But Harriet had already wobbled to her feet

110

and was doing her best to put the 'Great' back in 'Great Britain'. It wasn't a speech so much as a cookery demonstration and on a little table set out in front of her she proceeded to make a red jelly. It was just like *Playschool*, especially when she produced a ready-made one from the depths of her costume and threw it at the audience with a triumphal cry of, 'Eat more jelly!' People ducked, Jugsy got to his feet in alarm, and Slime sucked in his breath, but the jelly was only foam on a paper plate, and it made a harmless squashy landing in the middle of 3M. Harriet followed this by delving into her costume again and producing a few jelly packets which she threw among the juniors, who at once started fighting for them. 'First years, *please*,' Jugsy protested as the little ones dived for the jelly and turned into a wiggle of pink legs and grasping hands. 'Please, no eating in the school hall, I must *insist* . . .' But Slime indulgently flapped him down as Harriet shook and wobbled her way off the platform to a great round of applause, though his smile, Baz noticed, was becoming rather fixed. Was he having second thoughts, perhaps, about his great election idea? There was certainly a lot of noise now, in the Anderson Hall, and the audience was very restless. They'd enjoyed Harriet's act enormously. Was Cliff Turner going to outshine her?

No chance. He only spoke for half a minute, obviously frozen with nerves and simply trotting out his usual spiel about Cliff Richard that everyone had heard dozens of times before. The only good moment was when he whispered to someone at the side of the stage, 'Let it go,' and the huge hall speakers bellowed out the first few bars of 'Living Doll' before Jugsy disappeared behind the curtains and had the tape recorder switched off. Even though Cliff had shown up rather pathetically, he got a very big clap as he trailed droopily off the platform, and his supporters, all with hair sleeked back and wearing white plastic teeth from the joke shop in the new precinct, broke into 'Congratulations' loud and clear, before Jugsy, who seemed to have taken on the role of an extremely grumpy compère, for the morning's proceedings, told them that that was 'quite enough' and the election speeches must 'proceed'. He was making it abundantly clear that he disapproved of the whole time-wasting business. Not all the staff did though. Mr Slack had joined in with the singing of 'Congratulations', and The Cow had definitely been seen eating a jelly cube.

It was Polly's turn next, and to Baz's surprise, he made rather a mess of his speech. It was just too long and earnest for the fizzy, semi-hysterical mood of the listeners, who definitely wanted to be entertained now. People soon started to yell, 'Boring!' and, 'Get off the stage!' Nobody shut them up, Baz noticed, not even Jugsy, which was interesting, and certainly not fair. They must be nervous of Polly because of the Pullen's Field issue.

'Greens stand for a cleaner environment and a healthier earth!' he announced, raising his voice rather desperately above the growing din. It was getting increasingly difficult to make himself heard, over all the heckling.

'Wash your face, then!' a boy yelled and everybody laughed.

'Did you know that Pullen's Field is going to be concreted over and made into tennis-courts?' he carried on bravely.

'So what!' somebody shouted. 'Anyone for tennis?' And Slime exchanged a sharp look with Jugsy.

'Well, it *is*, and it means the total destruction of a valuable, natural habitat, a home for mammals and birds of all kinds. Do you really want that?'

'Yeah, we want birds!' the hecklers yelled. 'Bring on the birds! Bring on the birds!' You couldn't hear Polly now, people were laughing so much.

He was obviously confused. It was clear that he'd not reckoned on this happening. He'd thought he had a lot of support in the school and that they'd listen to him quietly. Baz saw him stuff his notes into his pocket, having retained just one of his many scraps of paper.

'Let me end with a line of poetry,' he said. He still looked very determined, but his voice was definitely wavering. Baz was willing him to stick it out, and not to depart ignominiously, like Cliff Turner, or worse, burst into tears. He looked as if he might.

'Oh, Gawd,' someone said, in a loud stage whisper, 'not *poetry*.'

'"Let them be left, wildness and wet,"' said Polly. '"Long live the weeds and the wilderness yet!" – that's Gerard Manley Hopkins by the way,' and he stuffed his paper into his pocket.

'And wet's the word!' a boy yelled. 'Get off the stage!'

Polly did, pushing his way past Baz with a mouth that was definitely trembling, and a face that had turned fiery red under the green make-up. He'd blown it. He'd just not been prepared for them all to be so hostile, and he'd blown it. Slime clapped politely and Baz joined in, followed by the juniors, who were still wide-eyed and adoring at the sight of this amazing green man. Unenthusiastically, the rest of the school clapped limply. Baz couldn't help wondering whether Polly wouldn't drop the Pullen's Field issue now. If he did, they could join forces. But it was obvious who would have to lead. In front of a difficult crowd like this Polly had proved a nervous, ineffectual speaker. He'd been right about himself. A little glamour was needed, and for all his cleverness Polly hadn't got . . . what did people call it? . . . *presence*.

Julius Malin had though, and his short effective speech for Cut Above was listened to with great respect, partly because Jugsy threatened to empty the hall if people didn't calm down, but really because the speech was so well delivered. Not that there was anything new in it, nothing that people hadn't heard before, in the school playground, but what came out of Julius Malin was absolute confidence; it was exuded through the pores of his skin, it virtually seeped out from the polish on his shiny black shoes. You *had* to listen to him. Even Baz listened, though disagreeing with every word he said. He'd been wrong about the sheaf of notes. As Julius stood up he left them on his chair. Perhaps he'd memorized everything, but you couldn't *tell*, that was the point, and he spoke with such authority and weight. You felt that if you'd stuck with Julius Malin as the *Titanic* was sinking, he'd have somehow made sure you got hold of a piece of wreckage and were saved. Baz rather marvelled at him. Here was this boy whom he'd punched in the face on Day One actually convincing him, almost, that all his disagreeable Cut Above ideas were OK, and ought to be followed through. No wonder he was one of Slime's 'Golden Boys'.

'You may well be whispering "he's a snob",' he was saying now ('in conclusion', for he had made it clear that his speech was divided into three short parts and he only had to say things once because he said them in a way that made people remember), 'you may well be saying that Cut Above is a snobbish kind of idea, and a snobbish kind of party. Well, you'd be wrong. In voting for me you will be voting for the very best. At Bryce's we have the very best, so don't listen to anyone who tells you to chuck it all away with any of this "Common Man" nonsense,' and he stared hard at Baz. Baz stared back. Well, at least he was paying him the compliment of taking him seriously.

At the 'Common Man nonsense' bit, something unexpected happened to the choir, which was sitting in two rows on the platform, behind Slime and Co. and behind the election speakers. Several of Baz's supporters were in it. He recognized them from their trumpet T-shirts. On this special election day, Slime had decreed that party supporters could wear their leader's colours, not that many people had bothered. Most were in Bryce's green, grey and silver as usual. But there were a few Cliff Richard T-shirts in the hall, one or two green faces, a large number of Squeaky Clean people, looking mega-smart, washed and pressed, and quite a lot of trumpet badges and T-shirts too. What Baz hadn't been told about were the flags. When he turned round he saw that all his choir supporters had home-made ones, just garden canes with what looked like big men's white handkerchiefs tacked on to them and the trumpet design in yellow. They were waving them now, and softly chanting, 'Greens out, Jelly out, Slime out – VOTE FOR BAZ!' and they did it for the rest of Malin's speech, but not loud enough for Jugsy to say they were 'disrupting' anything.

Baz was delighted. He'd not known they had been planning this, or that he'd got so many fans in the school choir. 'Slime out', was a bit much though, and he was quite relieved when the chanting got too raucous and the headmaster said crisply, 'That's enough choir, carry on Malin.'

'So, I want a greater pride in this school,' he was saying as he wound up his speech, 'and that surely starts with appearance. Ask yourself this question: Am I a credit to Bryce's? Boys, does your hair need cutting?' At this point he looked once again at Baz who hadn't had a haircut for weeks, as part of his campaign for more freedom and individuality. 'Girls,' he went on, 'have you got holes in your tights?' There was much laughter at this question, but Julius handled it well, laughing himself, as if it were his own joke and he'd planned for a laugh here, all along. 'No, but let's be serious, and let's remember the old saying, "Fine feathers make ... fine birds".' 'We want birds, we want birds,' the hecklers started up again, but Julius ignored them, simply raising his voice a couple of decibels, 'The point is, that schools like Bryce's produce men and women who will be *leaders in their field*. Look at Sir Albert Anderson, who's given us the money for our new tennis-courts, and listen, friends, no one can be serious who suggests we turn *down* such a magnificent offer.'

'Hear!, hear!' said Slime, beaming broadly.

'It's important that every single person looks good – and *sounds* good,' Julius continued. 'You should be able to take a Bryce's pupil anywhere. *So*, correct speech is important too. I'm campaigning for even higher standards in this school. That means an excellent prefect system, a blitz on sloppy appearance, on poor speech, on bad discipline ... everyone in this hall has a duty to make Bryce's an even greater school than it is at present, and therefore, ultimately, a *force in the world* –

115

and that means voting for me, and for Cut Above! Thank you.'

There was deafening applause as Julius left the platform. Jugsy half rose to his feet in enthusiasm but a frown from Slime, who was clapping heartily, made him hurriedly resume his seat again. The staff must remain neutral in the election, of course, whatever they might think privately, but there was really no doubt as to what the Jugsies and the Banerjees, and the Prouts thought; they just went on clapping and clapping.

Baz was panicking rather, as he rose to his feet. He knew he couldn't match Julius Malin for smoothness, or for crispness of delivery. Nor could he sound like somebody reading the national news on TV. He didn't have the right accent. As Slime introduced him, he rapidly revised his plans. His was the Common Man Party, so that's what he'd *be*, just an ordinary person, talking about ordinary things. But the point was, they were the things that mattered to most people, deep down. So that was going to be his line, *sincerity*. But he knew he'd have to do a bit of acting, too. All good politicians were actors, his father had said that.

Abandoning his notes, he actually started by praising Julius. 'I can't match old Julius,' he said, trying to sound as casual and as low-key as possible. 'He's brill, we all know that.' Out of the corner of his eye, he could see Jugsy shaking his head over the slang; no doubt he didn't approve of the accent either, but Baz had deliberately gone very broad Lancashire for the oc- casion. Some instinct was prompting him to play on the fact that he must, in every way, seem *inferior*, to Julius Malin. It could reap its own rewards, this approach.

And suddenly he decided he was going to play the music first, not save it. 'I am not in his league,' he went on, 'so here's something that says what I want to say better than any words could manage. OK, Alice, let it rip will you.' At the tape recorder Alice fiddled over the controls, 'Come on, *come on*,' Baz was pleading silently. Jugsy, no doubt anticipating more hideous, illegal din, seemed already to be stiffening in his seat,

116

looking wary again. He might forbid them to play the tape if she didn't hurry up; he'd stopped 'Living Doll'. But just in time she managed to press the right switches and to adjust all the volume and balance controls, and the opening bars of 'Fanfare for the Common Man' filled the hall.

It sounded marvellous in here. Sir Albert's money had been enough to furnish the place as a proper concert hall, and big orchestras played in it sometimes, as Slime never tired of reminding them. Baz stole a look at him as the great fanfare echoed around them. He had a funny sort of smile on his lips and he was stroking the side of his face thoughtfully. Jugsy was pouting. No doubt he felt it wasn't quite cricket to let Bradshaw have music when he'd denied it to Clifford Turner. But Baz had no doubt at all that the music had impressed people. They'd been all stupid and giggly before, only slowly calming down to listen to Malin, and only then because Jugsy had threatened them. But a silence fell as Alice faded out 'Fanfare for the Common Man', that special thick silence, the sort you could almost feel. It was the eager, hopeful silence of anticipation.

Baz remained very casual and smiled indulgently at his audience. 'That got you, didn't it?' he said with a little grin. 'I knew it would when I chose it, for two reasons. First, because it's brilliant, and second, because its about the Common Man – actually, it was written during the Second World War' (he'd put that bit in for Jugsy, who'd actually flown bombers in 1942, Granny B. had told him). 'Mrs Baxter played it to us in a music lesson and I thought, that's it, those trumpeters are playing our tune. So here I am, friends, just your ordinary common man speaking.'

People were definitely interested; he'd got them, he could tell. Undoing his jacket he stuck out his chest and pointed to the trumpet logo. 'Everyone supporting me is wearing one of these today. As you see, some of us are musical,' and he turned round and waved to the choir, who jiggled its little flags about and started chanting, *Jelly out, Malin out, Slime out*

— WE WANT BAZ!' until, nervous of breaking the spell he was weaving, Baz shook his head at them and turned back to the audience.

He said, 'You see it's all very well old Julius going on about fine feathers and that, but that's not *it* is it? Does it really matter what people wear, I mean now, *does* it? So long as they are comfortable in their clothes and they don't go around embarrassing other people? What's wrong with a pair of sneakers for Heaven's sake?' and he stuck out one rather beaten-up trainer, for inspection. 'What's wrong with the odd ear-ring? What's wrong with *colour* in life, and *choice*, and *individuality*? That's what Mr Lyme wants to encourage in this school, I know. He wants us to think for ourselves, don't you, sir?'

This was daring. 'I certainly do, Bradshaw,' Slime said with an icy smile. 'But do carry on, or I am afraid the clock will beat you, only three minutes, remember.' He obviously didn't like what he was hearing.

'OK. In my view all this palaver about uniform is a waste of time. *Inside* (and he tapped his chest), it's *inside* that matters, and inside I think we all want the same. Of course this is a great school, you don't need Julius Malin to tell you that, but if you vote for me you'll make it even better. You see, I want fairer chances for people. Let's not have prefects for a start, that's just a load of old cods. Governments like that have never worked, and they don't really work here. If we keep prefects, we'll be returning to the Dark Ages, you know, to the *slime* . . .'

Astonishment at this great audacity rippled through the hall, followed by laughter, and then by clapping. In the choir, the trumpeted flag-wavers began to chant, *'Slime out, Slime out!'*

'Will you be *quiet!*' Jugsy rapped in a strangled little voice. Officially nobody on the staff ever admitted to the headmaster's nickname, but everybody knew it, and some of them were stifling smiles now.

'I want a school council,' Baz said, 'so that *everyone* has a chance to say how this school should be run. I mean, who wants to be picked on because he's got a funny accent, OK, someone who talks a bit like *me*? Or because his mum and dad can't afford the *exact* uniform . . . like me? All that's a waste of time. We've got so much at Bryce's and yet, do you know, some people actually want *more*. Do we really need those new tennis-courts for a start? Let's stop being so . . . greedy. You know, some people can't play tennis because they can't actually *walk about* and they can't *walk about* because they've not got anything to *eat*. See what this says . . .' From inside his jacket he produced a folded poster which he opened up and displayed to the audience. He'd paid 50p for it out of party funds down at the Oxfam shop. 'Ever tried to eat a rat?' it said. He held it up, 'Well, have you?' The question was met with absolute silence, and Baz went on: 'We could raise some money for kids like this, couldn't we? We could stop whingeing about regulation shoes. Julius said Bryce's sends out people who are going to be world leaders. OK, make them the *best* world leaders, make them the leaders that care about things like *this*, and about people like *this*,' and he waved his poster about, 'about the forgotten people, the *common people*, *The Common Man*. Don't vote for Julius Malin, VOTE FOR BAZ!'

For a second or so nobody moved or spoke, then the applause began and the flag-wavers in the choir set up their chant, 'VOTE FOR BAZ!' which was steadily taken up all over the hall. Regulation sweaters were suddenly discarded, blazers thrown off, and the yellow trumpet logo seemed to shine forth triumphantly on all sides. Vanessa said she had managed to get a few more last night, but Baz had no idea she'd got so many, or that she'd given them out so quickly. How had she done all this? She was brilliant.

And so was Alice. Something told her that they needed the music again, the whole thing was taking off now. As it swept through the hall, people were stamping and clapping, and yelling, 'VOTE FOR BAZ!' The response to what they had just heard, combined with the marvellous music, was absolutely electric.

Then fighting broke out, somewhere in the middle of the hall, amid the third and fourth years. Afterwards, Polly said that he'd definitely seen Simon Speirs pushing someone over and that then someone else fell on them and a general scuffle followed. He believed it was to divert attention from Baz, that it was planned in advance as an emergency measure.

Slime ordered Baz to leave the platform. Jugsy switched off the music and Keith Slack waded into the middle of the rioters, bawling his head off, and calling them to order, delivering a few slaps. 'Leave the platform, Bradshaw!' Slime shouted. He had obviously had enough of his election for one day. The 'rowdyism', old woman Moncrieff had predicted had become reality, and he didn't like it, not in *his* school.

'I'm *trying* to, sir,' Baz shouted back above the noise, but he actually couldn't get down the steps. The junior mistresses were having a hard time calling the over-excited first years to order, because they were virtually camping out at the bottom of them, in the front of the hall, throwing jelly wrappers about, punching each other cheerily and vaguely chanting, 'Vote for Baz!' now and again, though they had enthusiastically clapped everyone else, too. 'Shut the stage curtains, Moncrieff,' Slime ordered. He clearly wanted some grand dramatic gesture to bring a speedy end to the affair. Jugsy scuttled off obediently to pull the necessary cords and, as the heavy green velvet drapes swished together, a sudden lull fell upon the school. This was *big*. This was *mega*. This was *Slimy-Slime* losing his rag.

'*Right*, that's *that*,' Slime said in a more controlled voice, obviously reassured that he could still command quiet in his school, and smoothing down the lapels of his gown. 'Now then, I would just like to *warn* everybody . . .' But what the warning was nobody ever found out; for at that moment something came crashing through a side window.

'Hey!' Keith Slack yelled, peering through the hole, then pushing open an *Exit* door and running into the playground. 'Hey!'

Baz, still at the bottom of the steps, stared out across the asphalt at two vanishing figures, pursued by Keith Slack, then down at the missile by his feet. It was a brick, and Tippexed in glaring white letters along one side were the words 'VOTE FOR BAZ.'

12

Alex and Kev, though too short of breath to speak for a few minutes, were definitely pleased with themselves; at least, *Alex* was pleased. The brick had been timed just right, shutting up that pompous twit of a headmaster and bringing a sudden end to the whole daft proceedings. Basil Bradshaw had been coming down from the platform when Alex had chucked the brick through the window. 'Pity it didn't hit him,' Alex muttered under his breath, pulling ferociously on his cigarette.

Kev said nervously, 'I'd put that fag out, if I were you. If someone comes after us they might see.' His voice sounded very wavery and thin and he couldn't stop shaking. He was frightened now. They'd just been hanging about outside Bryce's Assembly Hall, for a laugh, listening to what was going on, when they ought to have been at school. He'd never thought Alex *would* throw the brick, he'd thought he was just saying it for effect, talking big as usual.

'Don't be *thick*,' Alex sneered. 'You saw him, didn't you, that guy who came after us, the fatso in the track suit? He just went back into the school. He didn't exactly make a big effort, did he? The only way he could have collared us was to jump over the fence and I reckon that would give him a major heart attack. No, we're OK. Just cool it, will you,' and he puffed on.

They were right in the middle of Pullen's Field, squatting down in the bit where there was a slight dip and where the scrubby trees grew more thickly, their tops all knotted together. 'Pity they're going to chop this lot down,' he said, stretching his legs. 'I quite like this place.'

'They'll *have* to chop the trees down, whatever they do with it,' Kev said. He was whispering, in case that PE teacher

122

did creep up through the bushes, and he couldn't stop his teeth from chattering. 'They'd still have to clear the trees, even if they were going to build houses . . .'

Alex didn't reply, and Kev got the feeling, not for the first time either, that he wasn't actually interested in the Pullen's Field issue at all, that he didn't really care that Mr White was out of work, and on the bottle, and that people wouldn't have anywhere to live, and all because of Bryce's being greedy. He just enjoyed making trouble, taking risks and getting away with them.

But that couldn't be quite right, because he suddenly dug into his pocket and produced a roll of leaflets, bright yellow, the kind Polly had for his Green Party. 'This is the next thing,' he said, peeling one off and giving it to Kevin. 'I got them run off cheap at Kwikprint. I know a guy who works there.'

'Jobs not Snobs', Kev read, holding the leaflet up towards the thin light that filtered down through the trees. 'Read all about the tennis-court scandal. Top school grabs valuable building land . . .'

'What's this, then?' he muttered, but he knew. Alex obviously wanted to go public now, on the Pullen's Field issue, get the papers involved, that kind of thing. It was his parents' influence, this was; the Brodeys had big mouths.

'They're to stick through people's letter-boxes and stuff,' he said. 'Here,' and he produced another thick yellow wadge of the leaflets from an inside pocket and tried to press them into Kev's hand.

'Oh, listen, I'm not sure . . .' and Kev turned away. This was getting too big. His father had already been down at the police station for making a row on Inkerman Street, and now Alex was planning something else, something *he*'d have to get involved in.

'We could go on a protest march, too. That'd wipe the smile off the face of that creep Slime. He wouldn't like *that*.'

'A march?'

'"Course. We've got a valid case, mate. "Jobs not Snobs",'

he read proudly, fingering the yellow leaflets. 'If you want to smash your friend Baz's campaign I reckon you couldn't do better than make a bit of a song and dance about it, in public. Don't you reckon?'

'Mm, s'pose so . . . anyhow, come on, we'd better get to school, or they'll be after us.' And Kev started pushing his way through the trees, towards the fence of the Comprehensive, where there was a convenient hole for squeezing through.

'Who cares?' Alex called after him, lighting another cigarette.

Kev pushed on. He was wishing heartily that he'd never set eyes on Alex Brodey now, and he hated his own weakness for not sloughing him off. Baz wouldn't have stood for it, or let him be pushed about by Alex Brodey; but then Baz wasn't his friend any more. That was the whole problem.

Back at Bryce's Baz was sitting outside Slime's study, waiting to be called in. He'd been there for ages, since the end of the 'extraordinary' staff meeting which had been held immediately after assembly. The whole school had had an extra long break, while the teachers talked. No prizes for guessing what about, he thought gloomily, inspecting his finger-nails. They'd been discussing the school election, talking about what had happened in assembly, and about what was going to happen next.

He was just sitting there, minding his own business, when Julius Malin appeared and sat down at the opposite end of the row of chairs, leaving three empty seats. 'OK, *be* like that,' thought Baz, and he started to hum 'Fanfare for the Common Man' very quietly, under his breath. In retaliation, Julius immediately began to sing the school song.

'Forty years on, when afar and asunder
Parted are those who are singing today . . .'

They sang it every Friday at Slime's grand mark-reading.

124

He obviously couldn't get enough of it, though it was a ridiculous song for a place like Bryce's. What did any of it *mean* for Heaven's sake?

> 'Follow up, follow up, follow up,
> Till the fields ring again and again
> With the tramp of the twenty-two men . . .'

It was all about playing cricket, he supposed. But how could a girl sing that? It wasn't fair. In fact it was *sexist*. He ought to have said so in his speech.

'You for the chop too, then?' he said.

'Not that I am aware of. I just have to see Mr Lyme about the computer room timetable, that's all. I'm in charge of it. My father's firm supplied all the equipment. Do you want to put your name down for a slot? After school?'

'No thanks. I'm not really into computers.'

Julius shrugged. 'Suit yourself,' and he started to sing again, but a bit louder this time.

Baz began humming again, a bit louder still, hearing that marvellous explosion of great glittering brass instruments in his head. The two boys hadn't looked at each other, or said anything, but it was definitely war between them. It was all in the humming and singing.

Then Slime appeared at the end of the corridor, huffing and puffing rather, and striding along very purposefully, in a flurry of black gown and sheaves of papers. In his left hand he carried the brick that had been thrown through the window. 'Stop that noise, you two,' he snapped. 'Right, Bradshaw, you first. Come in, please.'

As Baz closed the door on Julius he could hear him still singing under his breath,

> 'Fights for the fearless, and goals for the eager,
> Twenty and thirty and forty years on . . .'

but not so loud that Slime could actually *hear*. Typical that was, really, Julius Malin could easily be called 'Slime Two'.

It was a few minutes before the headmaster actually spoke to him once they were in the study, he was too busy fiddling with a personal computer at a side table, feeding in a blue disk and examining a display on the screen. 'This little chap contains school records,' he said, over his shoulder, quite genially now, as if fiddling with his pet machine had somehow calmed him down a bit. 'This disk goes from Ackroyd, J. to Cowlishaw, P. You're in the middle, so I'll just have to . . . Yes, that's it, scroll forwards, now then, ah yes, Bradshaw, Basil William . . . Hmm. Quite an impressive record you've got, young man,' and Slime left the computer and sat down in his big swivel chair with The Brick dramatically in front of him on his huge leather-topped desk.

'Thank you, sir,' Baz said politely.

Slime stared at The Brick, neatening up a block of paper, and heaping paper-clips into a little pile. 'Pity you and Julius Malin should be at daggers drawn, don't you think?' and he gently pushed The Brick forwards a few inches.

'Do you mean the election, sir?'

'In a manner of speaking, I do, yes, Bradshaw.'

'Well, we're not really, sir, but an election's a kind of fight, isn't it? I mean, it's got to be. It'd be no fun otherwise.'

'Hmm, *fun* . . .' Slime tapped the side of his nose. 'From this morning's performance, I'd say the election had acquired certain . . . shall we call them *warlike* tendencies. I wouldn't call what has just happened "fun", would you? And I certainly didn't expect *this* to come flying through the window. You do realize that someone could have been killed, don't you Bradshaw?' His tone, as his fingers stroked the 'Vote for Baz' message on The Brick, was definitely accusatory. Baz found himself half-rising from his chair in protest, his cheeks burning. 'It was nothing to do with me, sir,' he said heatedly.

'Sit down, Bradshaw. I haven't said it was, have I? But somebody's got wind of our little election idea and I'd put my money on them being next door at your old school. Wouldn't you?'

'I'm not a betting man, sir,' Baz said smartly, trembling rather, at his own daring. This was one of Dad's sayings; it was better than telling a lie. He had no doubt who was responsible for the broken window. If only his father was here. He'd know exactly how to deal with Slime.

'Don't be impertinent, Bradshaw,' said the headmaster.

'I'm not, sir, honestly, but listen, I don't know anything about The Brick,' though he had seen those two boys pelting away towards the Comprehensive, one little and skinny, one broad and squat, like a pugnacious bulldog. *Kev* and *Alex*, he'd swear on it.

He said, resuming his seat, 'You want me to give up the election, don't you, sir?' He knew that was why the head had called him in. Granny Baxter had told Polly, and Polly had warned him, as he was on his way to the study. Slime may as well come clean. But he didn't answer, merely tapped his nose again and flicked dust off The Brick, as if it were some priceless museum piece.

'You do, don't you, sir?' he repeated.

'In a nutshell, yes, Bradshaw. For the good of the school, I feel it would be easier all round. What do you say?' Slime had lifted up his face from The Brick towards Baz, but he was refusing to look at him. His eyes, a pale weak blue, were sliding all over the place, anywhere but Baz. And Baz knew why, he was asking too much, in fact he was asking the impossible.

He said slowly, 'Is *everyone* in favour of me backing down, sir? What about The C— Matron? What about Mrs Baxter? She fixed up the music for us. And Mr Slack's on our side too, he said he'd vote for me, given half a chance.'

'Did he now?' Slime said coolly. It was quite obvious that he didn't approve of Keith Slack at all. 'The teachers don't have a vote, as you well know, and although I cannot go into the personal opinions of my colleagues here, I have a strong sense that the majority would prefer you to stand down.'

Baz stared at him suspiciously. A 'strong sense'. That was weak, *weak*. It meant precisely nothing. His bones told him that Slime was lying and that the staff were split down the middle. He knew that anyhow, from gossipy Granny B., via Polly. He said quietly, 'You said these elections were about democracy. You said everybody had a right to say what they thought and to fight for it. You said that in assembly, when you first told us about the election.'

'I did indeed, Bradshaw.' Slime had coloured up slightly now and was pulling at his shirt collar as if he was suddenly too hot. 'You have a perfect right to refuse of course, and to your own opinions – not that I agree with your views on the way this school should be run, because I don't. But I would just point out –'

'OK, sir, I refuse,' Baz interrupted.

There was an abrupt silence and the headmaster stared at him for a long time with what looked like disbelief, opened his mouth, and then shut it again. 'You *refuse*?'

'I do, sir.' Even though he was shaking in his shoes Baz felt his voice sounded firm enough and he was standing firm. Dad would surely have been proud of him. Why on earth *should* he back down?

'Very well, Bradshaw,' and Slime opened some kind of glossy brochure on his desk, flicking through it as if he'd lost all interest, 'you may go back to lessons.'

This was unexpected. No attempts to persuade, no threats, no blackmail. What was Slime playing at?

'We'll leave it there,' he went on, 'for now. But if there is any more damage to school property, I may call you in again to reconsider your position. You would be wise to do so in any case, for your own *good*,' and he leaned on the words, as he contemplated The Brick again.

'Sir, are you threatening me by any chance?' The minute he'd said it Baz cringed away, mentally. The words had certainly been in his mind, but he'd not meant to come out with them.

'Don't be impertinent, Bradshaw,' Slime said once again, icily. 'At Bryce's we do not threaten, we merely . . . advise.

Now, ask Julius Malin to step inside, will you ... And Brad-shaw,' he added, as Baz went to the door and pressed down the handle.

'Yes, sir?'

'These school records of yours have set me thinking. Your father was an exceptionally brave man. Would *he* have been proud of what happened this morning, do you think?'

'Goodbye, sir,' said Baz and he left the room. He didn't care how 'impertinent' he sounded. He *wouldn't* be forced to talk about his father. Slime could expel him first.

'You did well this morning, Malin,' the headmaster told Julius, as he looked through the immaculate timetable he'd drawn up for the computer room. 'Pity about that silliness at the end. You wouldn't know who is responsible for this?' and he prodded at The Brick. 'It's maddening, but they got away. We were all too busy concentrating on the little ones. Someone could have been seriously injured.'

Malin said coyly, 'I suppose it's those louts at the Com-prehensive again.'

'*Louts*?' Slime frowned. 'Language Malin, language,' he murmured, but not too critically, the boy felt. The head rumin-ated. Moncrieff was right perhaps, about this boy. He *was* splendid, a fine all-rounder, certainly Oxbridge material, but sometimes he rather overstepped the mark, was just that bit too familiar. 'I don't imagine Mr Greaves would be too pleased to hear his pupils described like that.'

'But they are, aren't they, sir? Look what they keep doing to the perimeter fence. Someone has been over it with aerosols again.'

'Really?'

'Yes, last night. It looks fresh. Haven't you seen it, sir?'

'No, I came in at the side entrance this morning.'

'Well, I'm just saying, sir ... we didn't have any of that kind of thing before Bradshaw came. Someone's trying to make trouble for him, I think.'

Slime looked thoughtful. 'You may be right, Malin. I must have another word with Mr Greaves, next door. Now then, this timetable of yours looks extremely professional . . . oh, no, Thursday afternoons are out, because of Senior Orchestra. Let's see . . .'

A phone rang in the outer office and Mrs Woods, the school secretary, put her head round the door. 'Could you have a quick word with Melissa Sanderson's mother, headmaster. She says it's urgent,' and she pulled a face.

Slime scowled. 'Not again, I . . . oh, all right. Hang on here for a minute, will you, Malin? I'll take it in Mrs Woods's office. Then we can have another think. Here, have a look at this, while you're waiting. It's going to be Maths, isn't it? I hope you'll try for Cambridge.'

He slid a fat 'University Guide' across the desk and went off into the adjoining room where Mrs Woods sat typing, and shut the door. But Julius didn't open the guide. His eyes were wandering, first to The Brick, then to the headmaster's computer on the sidetable. It *was* an old-fashioned affair, steam-driven, more or less. Now that Dad had kitted out the new block he was trying to persuade Slime to get something better than this for himself, but as usual the next phase all depended on fund-raising.

Through the wall, in Mrs Woods's office, Slime's voice droned on. Julius twiddled his thumbs impatiently. He was worried. Basil Bradshaw had surprised him with his performance at this morning's election assembly. He'd been very crude, but very effective, and although Julius had won quite a lot of support himself, he felt in the end the school had really been more behind Bradshaw. That brick coming through the window had been a kind of blessing in disguise because it had forced matters to end in disarray, diverting attention from Bradshaw's growing success and from the increasing attraction of the Common Man Party. Using that Oxfam poster had been brilliant.

He should have spoken last, not Bradshaw, but they'd drawn lots for it and Bradshaw had won. There was another reason to worry too. Everyone had been going round doing opinion polls this week, and all the latest figures suggested that Bradshaw was neck and neck with Cut Above. After this morning there must be a serious possibility that he would get ahead. He was definitely popular, especially with the juniors. It was sickening that such a crude, working-class type might actually end up representing Bryce's and all it stood for. Bryce's: the place where his father had been educated, and his two uncles, and his grandfather. *Grandfather*. What on earth would he have thought about the Common Man Party? He'd turn in his grave if he knew . . .

He could still hear Slime on Mrs Woods's phone. Next to The Brick was a small stack of blue computer disks. Julius leaned forward and picked off the top one, reading the label, 'Ackroyd, J. to Cowlishaw, P.' it read. His heart fluttered slightly. Ackroyd, J. was a boy in the Upper Sixth and Cowlishaw, P. a girl in the second year. So Bradshaw's records would be on this, if these disks represented the whole school. All the information would be transferred to hard disk when the rest of the equipment was installed by Dad's firm, but that would only happen when someone came up with the money. Until then, Slime was obviously using his own small computer, here in the safety of his study. Apparently the staff came in and consulted it from time to time. He couldn't really store this kind of information anywhere else. Boys like Julius, who understood computers, could easily break into such a simple system and get access to very private information. It would be as easy as A, B, C . . .

The computer was already switched on and the screen display was flashing a message 'Insert disk and press return'. With shaking fingers Julius slid the blue plastic square into position, pressed the necessary buttons and scrolled the illuminated display forwards till he reached the 'Bs'. *Barker, W., Benson, P. H., Birtleshaw, M., Bradshaw, B. W. BRADSHAW*, he read at last, *BASIL WILLIAM. Son of William Bradshaw and Helen*

Bradshaw. Father's occupation . . . But just as he was settling down to examine the entry, he heard clicking and pinging noises from the master telephone on Slime's desk, the head's voice in hearty booming exchange with Mrs Woods, the interconnecting door being opened . . .

He leapt away from the little computer, only just managing to resume his seat by the desk when Slime came in.

'Sorry about that, Malin. Now then, let's have another look at this schedule of yours.' But then he noticed the bright yellow cursor still flashing on his computer screen. He leaned over and snapped it off. 'Mustn't leave the thing on too long, I gather. It might take over the world . . . Thought I'd switched it off actually, must be seeing things . . .' and he smiled genially. '*Malin?* Are you with me? You look miles away. Well we can't use Thursday afternoon because of Orchestra. What I suggest . . .'

Julius, not listening, *was* 'miles away'. He had seen something extraordinarily interesting on that computer screen, something useful, and something that didn't square at all with what he'd heard so far about Basil Bradshaw. The minute he got away from Slime he must write it all down. The Common Man supporters could be in for a very big shock.

13

Sir Albert Anderson, wrapped snugly in a tartan rug in the back of his Daimler, was looking forward to his sherry, and then to his lunch. They always looked after him when he came to Bryce's, and so they should. He'd given them enough money over the years, new labs, swimming-pool, that school hall, now these extra tennis-courts. It was all because of him and because of Anderson's Wire, the company he had built up from nothing.

His stomach rumbled. He was an angry man generally, and at this moment he was angry with his wife Phyllis because she'd put him on a diet. No more rich food, she'd said, and definitely no alcohol. He was getting much too fat. She was a wise woman, though, it was because of her that he'd been generous to Bryce's. They'd not had any children of their own, and so they'd got no grandchildren either. The least they could do, she'd argued, was to help his old school, the place to which he owed so much, the place he'd come to in 1931, as a scholarship boy, his shoes patched by his father with bits of old leather, to keep them together. Humiliating. You never forgot things like that.

Emerging from the rug, he contemplated his highly polished toe-caps with satisfaction, then the distant view of Bryce's as the chauffeur slowed down to turn in at the gate. In the autumn sunshine the whole place looked a picture with its bright flower-beds, its clipped green lawns sweeping down to the road, the rolled gravel drive, without a speck of litter in sight, the flag fluttering over the old clock tower. Lyme often flew the flag, usually on the official birthdays of great personages. But secretly, Sir Albert liked to think that it was sometimes flown for him.

'Slow down, will you, Colin.' Leaning forward suddenly he tapped the chauffeur on the shoulder, pressed a button to open the rear window and peered out. The whole length of the long larch-lap fence, renewed last year, and another thing he'd paid for, had been defaced with aerosol sprays. He couldn't read the small slogans without his glasses but the bigger letters were plain enough. 'Bryce's is Rubbish' he picked out, 'Bryce's stinks' and biggest of all, and all over the place, the curious slogan, 'Vote for Baz'. At one end of the fence an elderly man in brown overalls was attempting to get the paint off with sandpaper, water and a scrubbing-brush.

Sir Albert thrust his head out. 'What's all this about then, Barraclough? And who's "Baz", for Heaven's sake?'

The old man shrugged rather wearily, and put down his scrubbing-brush. 'Dunno, Sir Albert. It's kids from next door again, I suppose. It's this election lark. Shouldn't be allowed, if you want my opinion. It's me as has to clear up, every time, and this is the worst yet.'

'Mmm. I'm on my way to lunch, I'll have word with Lyme,' and Sir Albert pressed his window button, returning to his tartan cocoon, but most definitely disquieted. Phyllis had said something about a mock election happening at Bryce's, she'd got it from her friend Doris at the Bridge Club, who had a son here. He'd not taken much notice at the time. Pity. He could have saved his fence. *Mock election.* The more he thought about it the angrier he felt. Time wasting. That's all it was, and he was going to say so to Lyme. There wasn't enough attention paid to the Three Rs these days; it was all 'projects', free expression and all that rubbish, and Bryce's was clearly no exception.

Slime was waiting for him at the main door of Big School, when the Daimler crunched to a halt. When he saw Sir Albert's face his heart rather failed him. The fat little man, squeezed into the straining dark City suit, looked even crustier than usual, and he wasn't an easy man to handle at the best of times, but bullying and impatient. Privately, the headmaste thought he'd done rather well, persuading him to part with this last big dollop of cash, for the new tennis-courts.

'Hello, Sir Albert, *hello*,' he said in his smoothest possible voice, pumping his hand. 'Lovely to see you again, as always. Lunch is all laid on, but I thought sherry first, with some of the staff . . .'

'Humph,' growled Sir Albert, barely responding to the handshake. 'Seen your fence, Lyme? What's it all about, this vote for every Tom, Dick and Harry business?'

'Oh, just a bit of fun, Sir Albert,' Slime said, ushering him into the school buildings. 'The children are holding their own elections. We thought it might kindle a keener interest in politics, and in view of what's been happening nationwide . . .'

'That fence doesn't look like "fun" to me, Lyme,' Sir Albert muttered grumpily. 'It'll take a lot of man hours, cleaning that lot off. I'd get the kids on to it if I were you, it's their *fault*. Don't see why Barraclough should be landed with it. Hasn't he got enough to do?' He'd been going quite fast, for someone so overweight, strutting down A corridor towards the Anderson Hall. He'd not seen it with the stage curtains installed. Phyllis had chosen the shade. 'Forest Green', it was called. It was meant to match the school uniforms. 'What is going on in there?' he said, peering through a glass panel into the vast pine-clad assembly hall. 'They're making a lot of row, aren't they? Why aren't they in lessons?'

'We have an extended lunch-break on Fridays, Sir Albert,' Slime explained patiently, 'and as they are so near voting day, I'm letting all the candidates use the time for their little meetings. Do go in, if you would like to.'

'Huh, sounds a right free-for-all, if you ask me,' Sir Albert grunted, pushing the door open.

'Carry on, everyone,' Slime shouted, sounding gayer than he felt, 'don't mind us.' But at the sight of the headmaster, standing there with the head of the school governors, who was also the wealthiest man in the town, everyone fell silent,

135

and the little groups of supporters edged away from their chosen candidates, staring at the open door.

Sir Albert went straight in and marched up to the broken window. A piece of brown cardboard, bearing the legend 'This side up' had been Sellotaped to it. 'What's this, then?' he demanded, tweaking up a corner and revealing the splintered glass.

'Oh, a spot of vandalism, I'm afraid. Outsiders of course, nothing to do with our children, no more than the fence. No, it's happening all over, I regret to say. Nowhere is sacrosanct these days.'

'A spot ... a *spot*? Plate glass costs brass, Lyme, and brass has to be earned. It doesn't grow on trees you know.'

The silence in the Anderson Hall was now palpable. Everyone was all ears, and greatly enjoying the spectacle of the headmaster being ticked off by this ludicrous, red-faced little old man, who scarcely came up to his knees. Slime could tell they were all lapping it up and he suddenly snapped, '*Carry on*, everyone, your time for electioneering is nearly up for today. Don't waste it.'

'*OK*,' said Polly defiantly, who was standing on a table covered with green crêpe paper, waving a bunch of twigs. 'As I was saying, there's absolutely no question, in my mind, of our going ahead with the new tennis-courts. Think of the loss of that precious bit of open land to the public. We've so little *space* in this town.'

Sir Albert, on the point of being successfully hustled sherry-wards by Slime, turned back. 'Hey, what's he on about?' he said. 'I'm paying for those new courts.'

'Oh, nothing, Sir Albert, absolutely nothing,' Slime lied desperately. 'Now, let's join my colleagues in the staff-room, shall we?'

But Sir Albert had marched back across the gleaming parquet floor and right up to the 'Green' table. Baz stood observing the scene with nervous admiration. Polly had done it on purpose. He *wanted* the old man to hear him.

'*You*,' Sir Albert said, cocking a thumb towards the door. 'Hop it, will you. Go and do a bit of work for a change, instead of all this speechifying, and get off that table, you'll break it. Many hands made light work in my day and the school fence needs washing down. Go on, and take all your friends with you. Go *green*,' he muttered, waddling back to the exit with Slime. 'I *went* green Lyme, when I saw my fence. I hope you *will* get it cleaned off. Organize a work party, get them to blow off a bit of steam. What on earth does that lad mean anyhow, *no new courts*?'

'Oh, just a bit of adolescent nonsense, Sir Albert,' Slime said vaguely. 'Now then, it *would* be a good idea to get the children to attack the fence, I agree. Just let's drop in at the staff-room shall we, everyone's so looking forward to seeing you again — and then I'll get it organized, before we go to lunch. Thank you for the idea, Sir Albert,' and he beamed down upon the old man's bald head; but his smile was like the grin on the face of a skull.

'Operation Scrub the Fence' was mounted for the last two lessons that afternoon, when most people had 'recreational activity', things like extra art or music, or else private study. Mr Banerjee, unwillingly, because it was his half-day, had been organized into rounding up what Slime vaguely described as the 'election people' and equipping them with cleaning materials. Now twenty or so of the main campaigners, candidates and supporters, pollsters, painters of posters, anybody in fact who Mr Banerjee had been able to lay his hands on, were trudging after him down the main drive of Bryce's, variously arrayed in art overalls, cookery aprons or simply polythene sacks tied round their waists with string. Mr Banerjee, who was always immaculate in his own appearance, had been careful to ensure that the expensive school uniforms were protected from what was bound to be a messy business. Otherwise he anticipated shoals of letters from irate parents.

Baz, wearing a flowery baking apron which looked as if it

belonged to someone twice as wide as Alice, was annoyed at the interruption to his day. He was missing an important swimming practice with Mr Slack; accordingly, he dragged his feet. He supposed Sir Albert was right saying it wasn't fair for Mr Barraclough to clean the fence, but was it fair for *them* to do it? Why not wait until the real culprits turned up, until they were caught, red-handed? But Slime said all that writing on the fence was a bad advertisement for Bryce's. *Image*, that was all he cared about. Anyhow, it said 'Vote for Baz' more than it said anything else. Secretly, he was rather proud of that, it meant he'd made a real impact.

As the colourful flapping crowd came down towards the fence, he heard a noise. It sounded like people chanting in unison, vague cheering, then clapping. The area round the fence was clearly already occupied by someone else, it sounded as if they were having a meeting. Mr Banerjee broke into a run. 'What on *earth's* that noise,' he was saying. 'Stay in line, children,' he called back. 'I must investigate this . . .' But, of course, nobody took any notice. The minute the teacher moved, they moved too, and soon they were all in a huddle at the school gates, staring along the paint-splashed fence towards where Bryce's land ended, and Pullen's Field began. Kev was sitting by the two big holes where, once, Ridgeways had put up their building sign, unenthusiastically pushing pieces of yellow paper into people's hands as they wandered by, and Alex Brodey, flanked by a few other boys from the Comprehensive, was marching up and down the road with a placard on a stick. 'Jobs for the Workers', it said, and they were all chanting, 'Jobs, not Snobs!' He was giving out leaflets too, rather more purposefully than Kev.

Nobody was listening much. The whole thing reminded Baz of that pathetic little old couple who stood by the war memorial in the town centre, on Saturday mornings, talking about Jesus Christ; rain or shine they were always there, as the traffic swirled round. Nobody took any notice of them at all, they seemed to be talking about forgiveness of sins, and about

Christ crucified, to empty air. But they were gentle-faced and timid, people he felt rather sorry for. Alex was aggressive and hard-faced. Kev ought to get away from him. *He* didn't seem to be enjoying himself very much, anyhow, drooping down there by the fence. Perhaps he'd had nothing to do with the aerosols. Or that brick. Baz noticed that he was wearing an outsized lapel badge, obviously home-made. Scrawled across it were the words 'Baz is Rubbish'. They exchanged covert glances, then both looked immediately away.

A few people had gathered round, curious about any development like this, especially when it seemed to have been master-minded by school children, and Alex was trying to make them listen, as he doled out his leaflets. 'You see,' they heard him tell one woman, 'this school's going to build tennis-courts on this bit of land, but it's already been set aside for housing. Here, take one of these. Read about it, and write to your MP.'

His victim, a crumpled-looking woman with a child squashed into a buggy, took a leaflet from him, murmuring vaguely, 'It's disgusting what's happening now. There's nowhere for the kiddies to play. It should be turned into a park, I think.'

In spite of what they'd been told, everyone had edged forwards, to see what was going on. Polly said, 'That's exactly what I think, madam. Do you vote Green, by any chance? I could send you some information, if you'd like to give me your address?'

'I don't know, I'm sure,' the young woman giggled, giving Alex's leaflet to the toddler in the buggy, who promptly started to eat it.

Alex came up mutinously to Polly and pushed him in the stomach with his placard. 'Here, you, clear off! You're interrupting a meeting.'

'Clear off yourself,' Polly said, pushing back. 'It's a free country.'

'*Silence*, everybody!' Mr Banerjee, his gown swirling round his legs, swooped down and split the two boys up, holding out his arms like a policeman on traffic duty. The little crowd disintegrated, but there were definite noises of dissent. 'Who does he think he is?' someone muttered. And someone else said, 'Who's *he* when he's at home, all done up like a dog's dinner?' Trust Mr Banerjee to come fence-cleaning in his *gown*, Baz was thinking in embarrassment. He had an overdeveloped sense of his own dignity. Quite a few of Bryce's teachers suffered from that.

'What do you think you are doing, mate?' Alex muttered, trying to stand his ground, as Mr Banerjee proceeded to hustle him along the pavement, towards the Comprehensive.

'I'm simply getting you off my land, young man. This is private property now, and that includes the pavement. We have come here to attend to our perimeter fence. Right children, spread out and I'll give you your instructions.'

But Alex wouldn't budge. 'Excuse *me*, but you're wrong. The Pullen's Field deal's not actually through yet. The documents haven't actually been signed. Ask my mother; she checked up.'

'That's right,' Kev said, speaking up for the first time. 'When a deal like that's been clinched, it's always in the papers, and it's not been, not yet.'

For a minute Mr Banerjee said nothing. The small crowd was listening and looking disapproving. Baz thought how silly the Bryce's lot looked, with their pinnies and their scrubbing-brushes.

As the teacher stood there uncertainly, a young man in a camel trench coat emerged from the crowd, presented him with a white business card, took out a notebook and whispered something in his ear. This really seemed to enrage Mr Banerjee. 'Absolutely *not*!' he protested loudly. 'No interviews of any kind. Come on, children, back to school, and he tried to reorganize them into some kind of crocodile. But we'll be back,' he thundered in Alex's direction, as, laughing and jeering, Alex began to pace the pavement again, with his placard.

'Jobs, not Snobs . . . Jobs for the Workers . . .' Baz heard the feeble chant being resumed as he trailed after the defeated army of cleaners, a furious Mr Banerjee at the helm. Who *was* that man? The teacher hadn't been able to get the children away from him quick enough. He seemed almost frightened of him, and as a result Alex Brodey had won.

He soon found out, because when he was half-way up the drive, kicking disconsolately at the gravel and thinking with pain about Kev, crouched unwillingly by the fence and how their eyes had met, the man came after him and pulled him into the cover of a great redwood tree that hung over the drive, a tree as broad as an elephant's legs. Unnerved, Baz tried to shake him off.

'It's OK. It's *OK*,' the man reassured him. 'I just wanted a quick word with you. Look, here's my card.'

Baz read it. 'Nick Train', it said, 'Pennine TV'.

'You're Baz Bradshaw, aren't you?' he said, flashing a quick toothpaste smile, 'The boy who's running for the Common Man Party, in Bryce's School election?'

'Yes, yes, I am,' stuttered Baz. 'But how did you know?' and tried to hand the card back.

'No, it's OK, I want you to keep it. Jack Pollitt is a mate of mine down at Pennine. You know his son, Ed, don't you?'

'Oh, yeah. Polly. He's thinking of joining my party actually. He made a mess of his first big speech, he's losing votes.'

Nick Train smiled knowingly. '*Really*? That's not what I heard exactly. I thought he'd persuaded you to join *him*.'

'Depends on how you look at it, doesn't it?' And Baz folded his arms stolidly.

The young man stared at him thoughtfully, then grinned. 'Fancy doing a spot of telly? For Pennine?'

Baz stared at him. '*Honestly*? You kidding?' It'd be marvellous to go on television and have a chance to talk about his party. That really *would* be the big time.

'I'm serious,' Nick Train said. 'Listen, we'd like you on *Young Voices*. It's the 5 o'clock teenage slot. It'd have to be tonight, though, we're filming in the town centre. Can you make it?'

Baz thought rapidly. He'd got another election meeting

arranged in Alice's garage. Polly was coming, to see if they couldn't reach some arrangement about the Greens. It was very important, but *TV* . . . he mustn't pass up such an opportunity.

'I'll do it,' he said at once.

'Great. Be there at a quarter to five, town hall steps.'

'Will you pay my expenses?'

Nick Train laughed out loud. 'Sure. Bus fare, new hair-do, . . . anything else?'

'Eh? Well, I'll send you an invoice,' Baz said cheekily, as the reporter turned away.

'*Bradshaw!*' It was Mr Banerjee, who'd come looking for him. The reporter dodged behind the huge redwood as Baz made his way up the drive. Perhaps, done out of the fence-cleaning, Mr Banerjee would send them all litter-picking in the playground now. Well, he didn't care. He was going on television. When he thought about it, his heart sang inside him, and he didn't feel a bit nervous.

Mum was right about him. He *did* like the glory.

14

He tried to slip off at a quarter to four without Alice seeing him. He wanted a bath or a shower before he went to the town hall. He ought to look his best. But everyone was crowding round a notice Jugsy had just stuck up on the special election bulletin-board in the main corridor.

He attempted to sneak past, but Alice spotted him. Sticking out an arm, she said, 'Look at this, Baz, Slime's offering *money* now, for information about the vandals.'

Polly examined the type-written sheet, then retreated in disgust. 'Oh, *yuk*. It's Uncle Albert again. "£50 for useful information" . . . Money, money, money. I might have known.'

'Who's "Uncle Albert"?' said Alice.

'Sir Albert Anderson, of course,' Polly told her, 'You should know, you've got an Anderson scholarship. He's the old twit who's put up the money for the tennis-courts, *and* the one who wanted us to clean the fence.'

'Do our scholarships get paid for by him, too, then?' said Baz. 'S'pose so.'

'Well, he can't be such a twit, can he? You could do worse things with your money.' Dad had thought very highly of Sir Albert, he remembered. He'd once fought for more black people to be employed in his factories.

'All I *mean*,' Polly said, obviously rather embarrassed now, 'is that it's typical of him to offer *money*. I mean look at this notice . . . *reward* . . . I ask you. How vulgar.'

'Everyone needs money,' muttered Baz. 'Wish we'd got a bit more, I do honestly.'

Alice, trying a tactful change of subject, said, 'Who do you think it is then, Polly, people from the Comp?'

'Dunno. It could be an inside job. You know, someone from one of the parties. They might have put their own slogans on the fence as well, just to mislead people.'

'If it *is*,' Baz pointed out, 'they definitely want me out of it. I mean it says "Baz" all over the place.'

'It could be Julius Malin,' Alice said thoughtfully.

'Ne'er,' Polly dismissed this with scorn. 'He'd never have the nerve.'

'Well, what do you think, Baz?' she persisted.

'Dunno,' he said, though he knew quite well what he thought. Surely it had been Alex and Kev running away from Keith Slack. And they'd been pounding up and down by the fence this afternoon too. Everything pointed to them. 'I'm going home,' he announced. 'See you at 6.30.'

'You said 5 o'clock, Baz,' Alice pointed out. 'My gran comes on Friday nights.'

'Yes, you did,' Polly said. 'I've got double Maths prep.'

'Well, I can't make five. I've got things on.'

'What things, Baz?' Alice was scuttling after him now, down the drive, trying to link arms.

'Just . . . things . . . and I'm in a hurry.'

He was proud. He wasn't telling anyone about the TV interview in case he made a mess of it. 'Mind your own business, Alice,' he added, as they walked to the bus-stop. 'You're too nosy for your own good, you are.'

'You wouldn't say that to Vanessa,' she pouted, stalking off.

'Oh, *Gawd*,' he thought, watching her go. She was off again. '*Girls* . . .!'

There wasn't time for a shower or a bath. He stripped, had a quick wash, and changed his clothes. He was going to wear his election outfit: tatty denims, trumpet T-shirt and ear-rings, but for once he was going to go the whole hog, and wear really big ones. He didn't know what time his mother'd be in, so he left her a note: *Watch ITV at 5 o'clock. You might get a surprise! Love, Baz.*

As he left the house he ruffled up his hair into a big black bush. He felt like looking . . . *wild*.

In front of the town hall he found all the paraphernalia of an outside broadcast: vans, thrumming generators, electric cables all over the place, a stall dispensing free coffee and tea, and people zooming about with files and microphones and clipboards, all braying at each other in loud voices. Everybody seemed to be called 'darling' or 'sweetie'.

The minute he hit the site, Nick Train grabbed him. 'Thought you weren't coming,' he said, rather less friendly than this afternoon under the redwood tree.

'Sorry, there was a mega traffic jam on Oldham Road. I had to get out of the bus and walk.'

As Nick outlined the interview and showed him a list of specimen questions, a make-up girl called Carole kept dabbing him with exotic-smelling lotions and powders. Then she back-combed his hair a bit, so that it looked even more wild. 'There you are, gorgeous,' she said with a giggle, kissing the top of his head, as she rushed off to do her next victim.

'Thanks,' whispered Baz. He'd be enjoying this, if only it wasn't so much of a rush. But two minutes later, they were *on*.

'Well, welcome to *Young Voices*, Baz,' Nick Train was saying, in his chattiest manner. 'Now, about this school election of yours. It's a great idea, isn't it? Organizing a campaign of your own, while people all over the country are getting ready to vote. But how is it going, exactly?'

'Pretty well, so far,' Baz said, though rather diffidently, trying to look into the camera as Nick had instructed him, but finding that his insides were suddenly snaking up and down with nerves.

'You don't sound too happy, Baz. Tell me more.'

Baz considered, 'Well, Bryce's — that's the school I go to — you know, the big place on Stockport New Road . . .'

'I know, I know.'

'Well, it's very, er, *traditional*.' He grinned, 'I think I've given them a bit of a shock though.'

'I'm sure you have –' and Nick sent one of the gigantic ear-rings swinging. 'I must say, I like your brassware. Part of the school uniform, is it?'

'You're joking,' Baz said ruefully. 'As a matter of fact, that's one of the things my party wants to change: the way the place is run. I mean, teachers don't wear a uniform, do they? I'm all for individuality, myself, doing your own thing.'

'And how does your headmaster view this, Baz?' Nick glanced down surreptitiously at his notes. 'Mr Lyme?'

'Oh, he's not happy, he's not happy at all. As a matter of fact ...' and Baz's voice trailed off into nothing as if Pennine North's thousands of viewers were all sitting right behind him, on the town-hall steps.

'Come on, Baz, speak up,' Nick pressed eagerly.

'Well, between you and me, he'd be happier if I dropped out. In fact, he's asked me to consider it. I don't call that democratic, do you?'

Nick Train clearly thought it prudent not to answer this. Instead he zipped on. 'How would you run the school then, Baz, apart from the uniform question?'

Baz thought for a minute, then he said, 'Well, do you know, I don't think I'd actually *have* a headmaster at all. He could get to be a dictator, couldn't he, like Hitler, or Saddam Hussein? No, I think I'd run the school on a rota basis. You could let the teachers have a term each.'

'I see. And what about the Green issue, Baz?' Nick consulted his watch. 'Time is racing on I'm afraid, but we can't leave that out.'

'I'm *not* Green,' Baz said doggedly. 'I'm Common Man, that's the name of my party, and we've got this fabulous music –'

'But, there's been some trouble, I gather,' Nick interrupted, 'about some waste ground the school has just acquired. People have been protesting, is that right?'

'Yes, it is. Pullen's Field. It's going to be made into tennis-courts, you see, and the point is, we've *got* tennis-courts. It was going to have houses built on it originally, and I personally think that's fairer, if it can't be left wild, of course. I mean, people have got to have somewhere to live, haven't they?'

'Quite. Absolutely. So you'd say Bryce's School was being a little bit greedy?'

'Yes, I would.'

'Well, I'm afraid that's all we've got time for. Thank you, Basil Bradshaw, Bryce's School, Common Man Party, and now for the latest regional weather, we go to Sandy McDougall.'

In the staff-room, where he'd been glued to the television set, Slime was more or less speechless. It was Granny Baxter's fault that he'd seen the programme. She always watched *Young Voices* on a Friday, before going home. She so enjoyed seeing the young people. But she'd had the shock of her life when she saw Baz, and for the next five minutes, like everyone else in the room, she'd been riveted to the screen.

As they faded Baz out in favour of the weather-map, Slime reached for the travelling phone. 'Get me Mrs Bradshaw's number, will you,' he ordered Jugsy, who immediately scuttled off. After the briefest of weather reports *Young Voices* were now being entertained by the Flintstones. 'It's 583119, headmaster,' Jugsy panted, having come back at a lick from Mrs Woods's office. Slime tapped out the number. 'Mrs Bradshaw? Lyme speaking from Bryce's School. I was just . . . I beg your pardon? Indeed I did. Quite a surprise. Yes, very. Now look, I really think we must talk. Could you call in and have a chat with me, say tomorrow morning? Oh, not till then? I see. Very well, Wednesday morning it is. Mrs Woods will confirm. Thank you.'

'Success, headmaster?' whispered Jugsy.

'Not exactly, she can't come till next week.'

'Can't or *won't*?'

'Won't, I suspect. She's like her wretched son, stubborn as they come. That boy's got to be stopped, Henry.'

Then the phone rang. Jugsy picked it up, 'Bryce's School? Yes. Yes. I'm not sure if he's available. *Darnley Examiner*, headmaster, to talk about Bradshaw,' Jugsy whispered, putting his hand over the mouthpiece.

'Tell them I'm in a meeting,' Slime said wearily. 'Oh *Gawd*, it's starting.'

Seconds later the phone rang again. This time it was the *Darnley Argus*. 'Look,' Slime said angrily, grabbing the phone from Jugsy, 'that interview with Basil Bradshaw has nothing whatever to do with me. Got that? Yes, well . . . and good night to you, too.'

'Mr Lyme really ought to calm down,' Granny Baxter whispered to Dr Prout, rolling up her knitting as she prepared to go home. 'Stress can bring on heart trouble you know, *and* cancer. Actually, I thought it was wonderful, having one of our children on television. And didn't he do well?'

'You were great on television, Baz,' Vanessa told him.

'Was I? Was I *honestly*? I thought I made a mess of it.'

'TV? When? Nobody told *me*.' This was Alice.

'I was on *Young Voices*. I didn't tell anyone apart from my mum. Thought I might blow it.'

'Congratulations, Baz,' said Polly, striding into the garage with a bulging file under his arm. 'And thanks for putting in a word about Pullen's Field.'

'Well, thank your dad, will you? It's because of him that Nick Train knew about me.'

'That's OK. I'd be hopeless on TV myself. But you're a natural.'

'Oh, come off it.'

'You *are*, honestly. Now listen. Do you want the good news first, or the bad?' and he opened his file.

'I'll have the bad,' Baz muttered. Since Dad, it was the safest policy, expecting nothing good to happen.

'Right. Well, according to the very latest Polly Poll . . . geddit? Polly Poll?'

'Oh, *come on*, Pollitt,' Jake moaned, seated at the drum-kit as usual.

'Yes, get on with it, Polly,' Baz grumbled.

'OK. Hear this. Cut Above is all set to win at the moment.'

'*No*,' said Baz defiantly. 'That can't be right. On Tuesday –'

'That was Tuesday, mate. People are fickle. Now, I'm not saying the TV interview won't shift the balance, but according to today's polls, and I've got four here, Cut Above's out in front. Malin was pretty impressive, you know, in assembly, and I know it's not your *fault*, but that brick with your name on didn't help.'

'But *I* didn't throw it!'

'I know, I know, but people are stupid, Baz. Now listen, you can't win on your own, *but* if you join up with me I reckon we'd win, hands down.'

'Are you sure?'

'Yes, absolutely ... Well, 99 per cent. I've done some predictions, here, you can look at them,' and he handed Baz his file. 'Go on, Baz. Go Green,' and he laughed.

Baz studied the figures carefully, and handed the file back.

'OK. Just suppose I *did* join up with your lot, it'd have to be *my* party.'

'Why?'

'Well, according to this I've got three times as much support as you. I'd have to lead it. And you said yourself that we needed, well, a figure-head. Pzazz, that's what you said I'd got.'

'I did,' Polly said humbly, flexing his puny muscles, 'and you have –'

'Let's have a look at that file again.'

'Feel free,' Polly said, handing it over.

Baz took a long time looking at all the facts and figures. 'No, I'm not sure I can, I mean, the Pullen's Field thing is crucial and people have lost their jobs because of that. How can I support the Greens, when you're against that building scheme?'

149

'This is why,' Polly explained: 'You've assumed they were going to build lots of little houses for people on that site, you know, "starter homes", cheap ones. They weren't. Oh no, they were going to be £300,000 jobs, *fabulous*, with jacuzzis and swimming-pools, the lot.'

'Are you *sure*?' Baz said suspiciously.

'Dead sure. I went to Ridgeways and looked at the plans. It'd have ended up a real Millionaires' Row, would Pullen's Field, if they'd been allowed to go ahead. Some Common Men they'd have been, living there.'

'I see,' Baz said, in a small voice. He had to admit that this discovery put rather a different complexion on things.

'*OK*.' he said decisively. 'Who votes we join with Polly?' Every single person in the garage put up a hand. 'You *do* want to win, don't you, Baz?' Alice clucked hennishly. But he stood there looking blank, obviously still undecided.

Scenting victory, Polly grabbed a spare poster and some felt-tips, 'What about this?' he said, striking out 'Vote for Baz' and writing 'Go Green with Baz' instead.

'Not sure,' Baz said. 'We'll have to negotiate, but basically we're agreed. We'll join up.'

'Great,' said Polly. '*Great*. I knew you'd come round,' and solemnly they shook hands, before everyone burst out laughing as Jake did a great roll on the drums.

Under the window Alex and Kev crept away. They'd hung round at the back of the garages most evenings and tonight they'd been rewarded for their pains. This time it was Kevin who spoke first. 'OK,' he said. 'That's *it*. I'm finished with Bryce's and I'm finished with Baz Bradshaw. You're right, he really *is* rubbish.' He could see their reasoning, about the expensive houses, but work was work and now his dad hadn't got any. What had happened to Baz's conscience about *that*?

'Great stuff. What's our next move then?'

'Dunno. You're the ideas man.'

'Yes, I am, aren't I?' Alex said with satisfaction, fishing out his cigarettes. 'I'll have to sleep on it, but now he's been on TV I think we ought to go for the big time, don't you?'

'You mean, something "mega"?' whispered Kev, remembering Alex's favourite word and feeling afraid suddenly.

'Yep. You've got it, pal. I mean something *really* "mega".'

15

Cut Above were sinking in the polls. Julius had predicted this. The minute he heard that Bradshaw had somehow got himself on television he knew that Common Man would soar in popularity, whatever the boy actually said. And, anyhow, he'd done quite well considering he was in front of the TV cameras; he'd been quite cheeky, quite bold.

Opinion polls were maddening, unpredictable things, you really couldn't trust them. One minute Cut Above were leading, then Bradshaw, then the Greens, then next day everyone had swapped places. Only this weekend though, Common Man and the Green Party had obviously sunk their differences, and joined up. Bradshaw was now including bits of Green policy in his speeches, Julius had noticed, and Pollitt had definitely piped down about the tennis-court issue. Now they had joined forces they were bound to win. Julius felt crushed. He wished he'd not been so confident at home, because his father was going round boasting about him already, about how *he* was going to win, to all his friends. A lot of them had been to Bryce's too. It was obviously unimaginable to these men, business people most of them, men of the world with excellent jobs and prospects, that a party like Bradshaw's Common Man could be taken seriously, let alone win. What was he going to *do*?

There was one thing, but he wasn't sure he dared. He'd got that information on Bradshaw written down. Not all of it. Slime had come back too quickly for him to read to the end but *enough*. If he made what he knew public, it would surely put the tin lid on any success for the Common Man Party. He could discredit Bradshaw completely. That computer disk ha revealed that he was an out and out *liar*, someone who curried sympathy for himself when he didn't actually deserve any. The story he'd spread round was disgusting.

Julius had told no one what he'd seen on that disk, not even Simon Speirs, his strongest supporter in the middle school, the boy in Bradshaw's class, and now he thought he *wouldn't* tell anyone. He'd just come out with it when the right moment came.

It came on the Tuesday, in the dinner-hour. People were having meetings whenever they could now; it was election week. Only three days to go and the school would be casting its vote.

Julius's supporters were getting on his nerves. They were losing heart. They'd all seen the polls. Edward Pollitt had rigged up his own 'Election Special' bulletin-board in General Area B and two or three times a day he stuck up a fresh notice. The figures were always slightly different, but nobody could ignore the general trend. Common Man, strengthened by the Green vote, was most certainly set to win.

Pollitt could be lying of course. Polls were often rigged in elections to persuade people to make their minds up the other way, and it would fit that Pollitt was a liar, because so was his new boss, the great Bradshaw. That was what Julius was going to tell people.

In the playground he climbed up on to his lab stool (decorated red, white and blue now, with a big cardboard school crest stuck to the front) and hailed everyone in sight with a proper electronically-operated megaphone. He was rather proud of his latest acquisition; his father had borrowed it for him. Other people had to make do with rolled-up newspapers; some, like Bradshaw, just yelled. Well, he'd stop yelling, perhaps, when he heard what Julius had to say.

Speirs was moaning at him again. He'd just been looking at Polly's 'Election Special' bulletin-board. 'It's no good,' he was saying, 'We're going right down. It was that TV interview

Bradshaw did. *Everyone* saw it. It's had the most fantastic impact, Julius. Honestly, I feel like quitting.'

'I'd stop worrying right now, if I were you,' Julius whispered down, steadying himself on the stool and adjusting his Cut Above rosette. 'I've got some extremely interesting information to give out, about Mr Bradshaw.'

'What kind of information?'

Even now Julius hesitated, when he thought of the enormity of what he was about to do. He muttered, '*Confidential.*' Well it was. 'But I think the time has come for it to be made public. Just listen to this.' And he straightened up, putting the electronic loud hailer to his lips. 'Cut Above, Cut Above!' he bellowed. 'Calling all supporters of Cut Above! It's less than three days to voting day and we need your full support. Calling all sane and sensible people to vote for Cut Above.'

Baz pricked his ears up and moved in the direction of the stool. Today was an 'off day' in his campaign. He'd been hard at it all yesterday, telling people about the merger with the Greens, and he decided there was such a thing as 'overkill' and that he'd keep quiet today, to let his message sink in. He reckoned that if you went on *all* the time, like the Cut Above lot, people might get fed up with you.

'Sane and sensible,' he whispered to Alice and Vanessa, who, arm-in-arm, were following him across the yard, 'that's a laugh for a start. Come on, let's have a bit of fun. I'm sick of Julius Malin boring on,' and he set up a chant, at the base of Julius's campaign stool, a chant which, to his surprise and delight, was rapidly taken up on all sides. 'Boring . . . *boring* . . . SLIME OUT . . . MALIN OUT . . . VOTE FOR BAZ!'

'If you'd all dry up for a minute,' Julius yelled, turning up the volume on his hailer to maximum, 'you might hear something to your advantage. Or are you all too stupid to be interested? I've got something here that might, just might make all you Common Man supporters think twice . . . A new view of Basil Bradshaw,' and he produced a piece of paper from his pocket and waved it at them. This was effective. The

154

crowd immediately started shushing everybody, and quietness fell. 'What's that?' someone called out.

Julius cleared his throat and handed his hailer to Simon Speirs. He obviously didn't need it now; he'd got them.

'OK. Well, for a start this Baz of yours, this leader of men – guess what his mother does for a living?'

'Prime Minister?'

'Stripper in a night-club?'

Baz tried to get hold of the paper. 'What *is* that?' he said angrily. 'Information about people's families is private. Where'd you get that from?'

But Julius waved it in the air, out of reach. He didn't need to read from it. He knew what it said by heart.

'It might interest you to know that the great Baz Bradshaw's mother cleans offices for a living. Want to be led to victory by someone whose mum smells of lavatory cleaner, do you? I mean, what sort of pedigree is that for Heaven's sake?'

Julius waited expectantly, still waving the paper. Baz was trying to grab the stool and knock him off, but Polly was holding him back. The crowd was definitely uncertain. '*Shame! Shame!*' shouted a number of the Upper Sixth, and several people shouted out, 'You're a snob, Malin.'

'Not only does she clean lavatories,' he went on, ignoring them all, 'she sees to old people. I expect she wipes their bottoms. Charming.'

'What if she does?' Baz was trying to push Malin off the stool now and his voice was tight with rage. 'Someone has to do it, you'll be old yourself one day. All this is irrelevant, Malin, and you know it. My mother works *hard*. She does a good honest job. Anyhow, what choice has she got? There's no one else to pay the bills in our house.'

'Ah well, I'm glad you brought that up, Bradshaw. I'm interested to hear that you prize honesty, because you are just a big hypocrite. You're a liar too. You went round saying your father was dead, didn't you? Oh, I *understand*, it was a sure way of getting sympathy for yourself wasn't it, for you

155

and your crackpot Common Man brigade? Well, hear this, everyone. You've all been conned. Baz Bradshaw, King of the Lavatory Brush, has been having you all on, I'm afraid, and when you know what I know you certainly won't want to vote for a person like that. His dad's not dead at all, and he's certainly not a hero. He's in *prison* for robbery with violence. And if you don't believe me, ask Slime.'

Baz hurled himself bodily at the cheerfully decorated stool and sent it flying. The loud hailer fell to the ground with a clang, rolling over and over on the yard and Julius rolled with it. Before he knew what was happening, he found Baz on top of him.

'I'll kill you for that, I'll *kill* you,' he was screaming hysterically, and, taking Julius by the shoulders he lifted his head up then sent it crunching back against the asphalt. Some of the girls started to cry.

'Don't, Baz, *don't* —' Alice screeched in terror. Jake Elder tried to pull Baz away, but received an almighty push which sent him staggering back across the yard. Polly muttered, 'I'm going to get the duty master,' and promptly disappeared.

All the time Baz had Julius on the ground he was screaming at him, 'I'll kill you, I'll kill you ...' The rest was incomprehensible to the terrified but fascinated bystanders. He was talking much too fast and his teeth were clenched tight in fury. 'Listen to him,' Julius panted, still struggling to throw him off, 'he's just an animal. Get back to the jungle Bradshaw, or join your father in the clink!'

Baz raised his fist and gave him a massive blow on the jaw, and the crowd screamed again, hearing, they were certain, the crunch of bone against asphalt. Then he suddenly found himself being pulled away from Malin and flung away like discarded rubbish. Keith Slack was kneeling over Julius, slapping his cheeks and shouting, '*Malin.*'

'Oh, my God, what have you done, Bradshaw?' he muttered, when there was no response and he undid the boy's collar and loosened his tie. 'Malin, *Malin!*' But Julius's face was the colour of ash, his eyes were closed and when the teacher touched his face, his head just lolled to one side, horribly.

'More coffee, Mrs Bradshaw?' Slime said. 'I feel like another. I'll just buzz through to Mrs Woods.'

'No, thank you, Mr Lyme. I'm supposed to be at work. I only asked for an hour off, I really ought to be back by now.'

'As you wish. But I'm sure you will agree, Mrs Bradshaw,' the head said smoothly, but with a certain steeliness creeping into his voice, 'that this affair is really very grave indeed, and that we must give it as much time as it takes. Would you like to ring your employer? You could do it from here.'

'No, thank you. They'll understand. I'd just like to get to the point if you don't mind.'

'Very *well*, then,' Slime said, in his most official manner, tidying up his desk and neatening up blocks of paper, paper-clips, phone, pens. 'Let's talk about the playground episode yesterday, shall we? I know this appointment was originally made for us to discuss Baz's future in the election, but in the circumstances —'

'Was it, Mr Lyme?' Mrs Bradshaw interrupted rather warily. 'I thought it was about the TV show. How to deal with awkward reporters and that. I've had several pestering me already. I'd be grateful for your advice on that one.'

Slime instantly changed tack. He'd imagined he could steam-roller this crushed-looking, sad, little woman into submission when Mrs Woods had first shown her into his office. Now he wasn't so sure. Did she really not understand the enormity of Bradshaw's violent behaviour, or was she being deliberately obtuse, to protect her precious son? He was now rueing the day that they'd ever let him into Bryce's. He'd caused nothing but trouble, with all his brains.

'Of course, of course,' he said smoothly. 'A knotty problem, I agree. Media people can behave quite outrageously, given half a chance. We *will* get round to it, I assure you. But first there's Julius. Mrs Bradshaw, I don't want to alarm you but the boy could have died.'

'Basil was provoked beyond *bearing*, headmaster. Everyone says so.' She stared ahead rigidly, trying to keep calm, trying not to give way to the huge inexplicable wave of emotion that was hovering suddenly, and threatening to engulf her.

'How was he "provoked", exactly, Mrs Bradshaw? How can you possibly justify the violence of your son's reaction? Knocking another boy to the ground, then banging his head on solid asphalt? He's still suffering from concussion, Mrs Bradshaw. He was unconscious for several seconds; thank God Mr Slack was there.'

Baz's mother suddenly got to her feet, and jabbed a finger at the headmaster. 'That boy had access to private information, headmaster,' she said, in a high strangled voice. 'He had seen confidential school records relating to my son and to my family, and he got his facts wrong. Now first things first. How did Julius Malin get *hold* of such information? That in itself is scandalous.'

'I'm sure I don't know, Mrs Bradshaw,' Slime said weakly, flicking a look sideways at his computer, and remembering quite clearly that discussion with Malin about the timetable, how he'd left the room to use Mrs Woods's phone, and how, when he'd returned, he noticed the machine was on. He knew exactly what had happened because he'd been to Malin's home last night to investigate. It was only because the terrified boy had confessed to breaking into the system that his father wasn't going to bring charges against Bradshaw and against the school. He'd judged it was more in his son's interest to keep quiet about the whole thing. But had Mrs Bradshaw consulted a solicitor too? She sounded as if she knew what she was talking about.

'You *do* know, Mr Lyme. Julius Malin's father has a computer business. He has supplied equipment to this school. Baz told me himself. And the boy's brilliant on them. It would be nothing to him to break into the school system and that's exactly what he did, isn't it? I must say, this is a really marvellous school, if that's the way it handles private information. If you ask me

158

you'd be better going back to the old method, of keeping a card index. At least you could lock it up.'

'Well, I'm sorry, Mrs Bradshaw, but boys will be boys you know,' Slime said feebly. 'Now about the attack on Malin . . . '

'We haven't finished with the attack on Basil yet, headmaster,' she countered stonily, '*Nor* on my husband. Basil's father was a fine man. He lost his life trying to protect someone: he was *shot*, at point-blank range,' and she sat down quite suddenly, covering her face with her hands.

Slime sat down too. 'I know, Mrs Bradshaw, I know, that terrible incident when they held up the building society. Listen, I've *tried* to talk to your son about it, you know, but he switches off. Matron's tried too. It's bad to bottle up your grief, we all know that, but we just can't get through to him. Of *course* Basil's father was a fine man, and believe me we have tried to get him to talk about that hideous day, more than once.'

'It's too soon, for him, Mr Lyme. It's much too soon. He *can't*.' And Mrs Bradshaw wept.

Slime went next door and ordered more coffee from Mrs Woods, leaving her to cry alone. But when he came back with the tray she was calmer. She'd wiped her eyes and was sitting with her hands folded in her lap. She said, 'I can see how Julius Malin made his mistake, Mr Lyme. The man who killed my husband was called *Braithwaite*. You could easily mistake that name for Bradshaw, on a little screen, if you were in a real hurry, and if you shouldn't have been looking in the first place. He's the one in prison, *Terence Braithwaite*; I hope he never comes out. And then this boy goes accusing Basil's father, when he's *dead* . . . ' She was fighting very hard not to break down again, and Slime leaned forward, touching her arm. 'I'm sorry, Mrs Bradshaw, I'm truly sorry. What else can I say?'

'Nothing.'

After a decent pause and the pouring of coffee, he said gently, 'May I go on?'

'Do,' she said stonily, 'There's nothing else to be said about what happened at the National and Provincial, I can't really talk about it either. I'm no help to Baz I don't suppose. I'm part of his problem perhaps.'

'Well, setting this truly appalling incident aside for a minute — and really I'm not blaming either of them about yesterday — I'm actually not very happy about Basil running in the election.'

Mrs Bradshaw sat up. 'Oh, why ever not? I thought it was all going rather well. He's in front at the moment, isn't he?'

'He may well be, Mrs Bradshaw. He may well be. But that television appearance was really most unfortunate.'

'What was wrong with it? I thought he had a good showing. He made me laugh. Get rid of the headmaster ... ear-rings ... *honestly*,' and for the first time, she smiled. But Slime didn't respond.

'The point is, he has undermined the whole ethos of the *school*, Mrs Bradshaw. Don't you understand? His suggestion that we should scrap our plan to have new tennis-courts, that's got me into real hot water with Sir Albert Anderson. He's put up all the money, and as it happens he was watching the programme. The point about the scholarship winners, Mrs Bradshaw, is that while they are *bright* — and they don't come brighter than your son, I assure you — they don't have ... how can I put it ... well, too much social awareness. Get my drift?'

'Not really,' Basil's mother said icily. She understood precisely.

'Well, with this Common Man nonsense, Mrs Bradshaw,' Slime went on, 'your son is actually, I hate to say it, he's damaging the image of the school. Now he's certainly got a lot of people on his side, I won't deny that, because he's run his campaign very well, and he's got ... you know ... flair but he's going in the wrong *direction*, Mrs Bradshaw, he's threatening our great traditions, everything this school stand for. Surely you hear what I'm saying? *Do* ask him to stand down, Mrs Bradshaw. If he won it would be deeply embarrassing. We have a problem with vandalism too now. I expect you know about that. Of course, it's not your son's fault, but they would seem to be, you know, former chums of his, from the Comprehensive. It just can't go *on*, Mrs Bradshaw,' he ended, rather desperately.

After a very long pause Mrs Bradshaw said calmly, 'Mr Lyme, my son's no threat to you.'

'I beg your pardon?'

'Well, if this school's all you say it is, it isn't going to be knocked off course by someone like my Baz, now, is it? I mean, he's only having a bit of *fun*, like they all are. He's at that age. He's just finding out who he is, that's all. I expect that's all Julius Malin's doing too.' she added, giving him a very direct stare.

Slime looked away. 'So you won't suggest he might climb down, for the good of the school?'

'I'm sorry, but I don't think I can, Mr Lyme. You see, his father was very interested in politics, really it's in the blood, and somehow – you know, I feel Baz is doing this for *him*. He's set his heart on it. And that incident yesterday, with Julius Malin, seems to have made him more determined, if anything.'

'So you're not going to co-operate with the school?' Slime, now standing, had suddenly shed any appearance of friendliness or sympathy. 'In a nutshell you refuse to co-operate with us?'

'In a nutshell, yes,' Mrs Bradshaw answered, buttoning up her coat.

Jugsy, watching her hurrying down the drive from the window of the Senior Common Room, was knocking on Slime's door in seconds. '*Come*,' said the headmaster imperiously, pacing the floor. He was astounded at the woman's refusal to co-operate.

'How did you get on with Mrs Bradshaw, headmaster? Did she agree?' inquired Jugsy eagerly, hopefully wringing his hands.

161

'She did not. "I refuse", was what she said. More or less.'

'I *refuse*?'

'I refuse . . . I think we've heard that somewhere before.'

'But what are we going to *do*, headmaster?'

'Henry, I have absolutely no idea. Mrs Woods,' he called out, 'could you come in here a minute?'

He needed his third cup of strong coffee, and it was only 10.30 in the morning.

16

That night, The Cow saved the school.

She was in her dressing-gown and on her way to bed, having said good night to the twelve 'country boarders' who lived too far from Bryce's to go home, except at weekends and who slept in a small dormitory off C corridor, when she smelt a funny, suspicious smell. She instantly knew that there was a fire somewhere and she went into action.

Bryce's was virtually deserted and nobody was near enough to shout to for help. It was Dr Prout's duty week, but he was right at the other end of the school premises, and Mr Barraclough was in his bungalow, down by the main gates, watching football on TV. Hitching up her dressing-gown she ran down three flights of stairs and pelted along A corridor, past the Senior Common Room, past the girls' lavatories, past the gym and up to the Anderson Hall, where she saw thick smoke snaking out from under all the doors. She wrenched the nearest one open, then immediately slammed it shut again. She could hear flames roaring inside, and the crackling of paper. The blaze must be *contained*.

Poor kids, she thought as she tore back along A corridor to the staff-room, and therefore to the phone and to the nearest fire-alarm. The election people had spent all afternoon in there, setting up 'stalls' for their last big drive before voting day on Friday. It didn't look as if much would be left of their efforts now. But how could a fire have started in the Anderson Hall? It was brand-new. Electrical faults often started fires like that, but they nearly always happened in *old* buildings . . .

Thanks to The Cow, the blaze didn't spread beyond the hall. Help arrived within minutes and all the firemen had to deal with were great heaps of charred paper and lumps of sodden cotton, the remains of the material so carefully assembled by the political parties, their posters and leaflets, their decorations and their free badges and T-shirts. The police came briefly and took a few photographs but said they would be back next morning to inspect the scene more carefully. Together with Dr Prout and old Mr Barraclough, Matron, still in her dressing-gown, waded gloomily through the wreckage, seeing if there was anything at all she could salvage to give to the children the next day. She felt sorry for them all after their marvellous efforts to decorate their stalls. In the middle of her poking about, Slime arrived, not at all grateful for her prompt action in calling the fire brigade, merely ordering her to inspect the country boarders immediately, to make sure they were all in their beds. He seemed angrier than she could ever remember. It was odd.

All was explained next morning, when people saw the Anderson Hall in daylight. Amazingly, very little structural damage had been done, though all the light fittings had cracked and the pine-clad walls were charred in places. But what had so angered Slime was something The Cow hadn't really taken in through the swirling smoke last night, the fact that every conceivable wall had been aerosoled in gigantic letters with the same three words repeated over and over again: BAZ IS RUBBISH. Nothing else at all.

At first Baz wasn't singled out for special treatment, nobody commented, not even Slime, though he kept popping in to oversee the clearing-up operations, on which the election groups were occupied all morning. It was a very subdued gathering indeed and it was a horribly messy business, decanting stinking, sodden rubbish into black plastic sacks, sweeping the floor, attempting, quite hopelessly as it turned out, to get the paint off the walls. That, announced Slime, was a job for professionals and *someone* was going to have to pay for it. When he said this bit, he looked straight at Baz. He definitely wasn't imagining it.

The police worked alongside the children. Nobody was supposed to know, but a very young constable let it out to Polly that they were almost certain the blaze had been caused by a cigarette-end. They'd found a couple of them, and a lighter. Baz actually saw them being put into a polythene bag and given to a superintendent in plain clothes. It was just like *Inspector Morse* on TV.

Everybody assumed that the fire meant the end of the election and that Slime would say 'Enough is enough'. It was one of his favourite tags; Jake said it would be carved on his gravestone. Baz wasn't letting himself think who might have been in, daubing his name all over the walls and starting the blaze, any more than he was letting himself think about his father. He had sealed the matter off in his mind. His suspicions were just too awful. To everyone's surprise, just as Mr Barra-clough was collecting together the bulging rubbish bags, Slime came back, with Jugsy this time, and clapped his hands together. Baz suppressed a smile, that was another thing about the head: he gave himself all these elaborate airs and graces but, to command attention, he always did that. Baz could remember it happening at his infant school.

'Several people have been asking me about the election tomorrow,' he said crisply, 'and I have decided it *must* go ahead. It will be low-key of course and there won't be any more speeches. Obviously this hall will be out of use for some days and we will have to transfer to the gymnasium, but I'm absolutely determined to show these terrible people that Bryce's won't be beaten, so there *will* be a vote tomorrow and, er, may the best man win.'

'Or woman,' muttered Harriet Weatherall, chewing on a piece of raspberry jelly that had miraculously escaped the flames.

'Do we know who the terrible people are yet, Mr Lyme?' Jake piped up cheekily. He'd quite enjoyed this morning. They'd missed double Maths and double Biology, the two biggest bores of the week. Really, the whole thing had livened

Bryce's up no end. 'Absolutely not,' Slime said heavily, 'and I really can't discuss it. Now finish up here will you, and then go and join the lunch queue. Thank you for your efforts everybody. Mr Moncrieff will you make sure all is left in reasonable order here, please? I must go and look after Sir Albert before our meeting,' and he stalked out.

The minute he'd gone everyone converged on Jugsy. 'What's Sir Albert come for, sir?' Jake said. 'What's going on?' A definite air of mystery and intrigue hung in the air now, like the smelly, dirty fug still left over from the fire. They all sensed that there were things they still didn't *know*. 'Are we really going ahead tomorrow, sir?' asked Polly. He'd not been excited by the fire and by the wrecking of their carefully prepared stalls; he'd been sickened. He and Baz had worked so hard to win and this morning it had seemed like the end of everything.

'We are, apparently,' Jugsy said, in an extremely low voice, and one which spelt disapproval. 'But I understand there are to be certain modifications.'

'What modifications, sir?' asked Baz. Jugsy wasn't happy, he could tell. He'd put his money on there being some kind of disagreement between him and Slime, not that they would ever know the details. The Cow had told him that Jugsy had his own private thoughts about quite a few things at Bryce's, but that on the surface, he always stayed absolutely loyal to Slime. She admired him for it.

'Yes, why is Sir Albert here, sir?' said Alice. 'He came last week, twice. He's always here.'

'I'm afraid news reached him about the fire and he's insisted on Mr Lyme's calling a meeting, with one or two, er, key figures. Bradshaw, you are to report to the headmaster's study at 1.30 p.m. Go and have your lunch and if I were you I'd wash your face too. It's filthy.'

It was absolutely no surprise to Baz that he'd been summoned to the meeting in Slime's study. *Baz is Rubbish* . . . How many times had that screamed out at him this morning, in dazzling white paint, from the walls of the Anderson Hall? There he sat, pushed into a corner of the room, perched on a hard plastic chair, facing Slime and Sir Albert across a vast expanse of polished leather which covered the headmaster's grandiose writing-desk. To the side sat Jugsy, and next to him The Cow. Standing up, with his back to the window was a policeman. The young officer met Baz's eye as they waited for Slime to start the proceedings. It was this constable that had asked them to keep their eyes skinned for anything at all 'suspicious' as they'd help clear up the mess in the Anderson Hall, anything the police could bag up and take away for analysis. Nobody had found anything, to their great disappointment. Nobody except Baz, and he was keeping mum.

Just as Slime opened his mouth, Sir Albert leaned forward, muttered to The Cow, 'Is this the boy?' and said to Baz, 'There could be money in this for you, lad. I've already offered £50 and I'm not unwilling to put up another £50. Come on, what do you say? Brass is brass. It's not to be sneezed at.'

Slime, obviously embarrassed by this crudeness, stood up too, towering over the red-faced, diminutive Sir Albert. 'We just need to know, Bradshaw, if you can tell us anything at all, if you have *any* inkling of who might be behind what happened last night. They got in through the broken window, of course, and two and two makes four.'

'What's that supposed to mean, sir?' He knew it sounded rude, but what was he meant to say? They were hinting that whoever threw the brick had wrecked the stalls and painted the walls too. And they didn't need to spell out that they thought the culprits were his old mates, and that they came from the Comprehensive. So far though, Mr Greaves couldn't have co-operated. Otherwise he'd surely be here, at this meeting, *and* the arsonists . . . Not that Baz could believe that bit of it; surely the fire had been an accident? They'd never have gone that far; someone could have been killed.

As if reading his mind The Cow said very gently, 'It could

have been terribly serious, Baz. People might have been burned to death.'

'And it's all got to be paid for, young feller, don't forget that,' chipped in Sir Albert.

'Not by me, it's not,' Baz answered belligerently.

The little man's piggy eyes bulged. 'I beg your pardon . . . ' he stammered.

'I said, "not by me". I don't go round setting fire to other people's property, Sir Albert, not even if my mother does clean lavatories.'

'What the hell are you on about?'

'Now, now, Bradshaw,' soothed Slime, in deep embarrassment. 'Nobody's accusing *you* of anything, but the facts are these – that since the election campaign started – '

'Bloody daft idea,' grunted Sir Albert.

'Since the election campaign started,' repeated Slime, 'there have been several attacks on this school. The fence has had graffiti sprayed over it, at least three times, and it's also been damaged. A brick was thrown through the window during the first big election meeting, and last night . . . well . . . we all know what happened last night. And you seem to be the *one* Bradshaw. *Vote for Baz, Baz is Rubbish.* Oh, it doesn't make sense at all, but you're the one everything seems to hinge on. Now, have you any idea why? Can you tell us anything *at all* that might help?'

'No, sir.'

'You're absolutely certain?'

There was a long silence during which Baz inspected every square inch of his shabby, non-regulation black shoes. Then he crossed his fingers, out of habit. When he was little he'd always believed that you wouldn't go to hell if you crossed your fingers when you told a lie.

'Yes, sir.'

Sir Albert snorted like a pig and Slime let out a long, slow, dramatic sigh.

'*Right.* Have you any questions for us, Bradshaw, before you go?'

'Well, yes, just one, sir.'

'And what is it?'

'Are we really still having the elections tomorrow, sir? Mr Moncrieff said we were.'

'That is correct, Bradshaw.'

'It's bloody *ridiculous*, if you ask me,' said Sir Albert, under his breath.

'But there will have to be, er, certain modifications, now,' continued Slime. 'No big speeches I'm afraid, everything rather low-key, other minor changes perhaps ... I suppose, at this late stage, I still can't persuade you to stand down?'

'No, sir.'

'Very well. You may go for now, Bradshaw.'

'Sir,' he said, as he went to the door, 'what are these "modifications"?'

Slime coloured slightly. 'Any extra information will be posted up in the General Areas, on the special notice-boards. You must consult those, Bradshaw.'

'That lad *knows* something, if you ask me,' humphed Sir Albert, making no attempt to lower his voice as Baz shut the door behind him. Out in the corridor, he pulled his collar and tie straight, aware that he was sweating slightly, through nerves. Then his fingers reached down into his jacket pocket, closing round what he'd found in the Anderson Hall, when they were clearing up all the mess.

When he went round to Kev's, that night, he was watching *Neighbours*. Nothing was different. If anything, the house was even more depressing: the same rubbish everywhere, the piles of washing and the sink full of dirty dishes, the same unpleasant smell. On the table was a row of empty lager cans. Kev sat slouched in a greasy chair with his feet on the mantelpiece.

The back door was open, and Baz walked straight in. He didn't much care whether Mr White was in or not, the way he was feeling, but he'd almost certainly be down the pub already, or else sleeping off a drinking session upstairs.

'What do you want?' Kev muttered, not taking his eyes off the television. 'Didn't hear you knock.'

'I didn't.'

Perhaps Kev had caught the slight aggression in Baz's voice, because he didn't try to chuck him out, he just flicked a wary, rather embarrassed look at him, then glued his eyes back pointedly on the screen; and they both knew in that instant that Baz knew who'd been into Bryce's last night.

Baz leaned forward, switched off the television, positioned himself at the table behind the beer cans and fixed his eyes on Kev. 'Hey, I was watching that, Henry's getting married in this episode.'

'Henry off!' said Baz. 'I've got something for you. I think it's yours anyhow.' From his pocket he took a small round packet wrapped in a bit of Kleenex.

Kev untwisted the tissue and took out the contents, holding it between his finger and thumb. His hands were shaking, in fact, he seemed to be shaking all over. Baz pitied him. He'd always been a very nervy type. How on earth had he ever got mixed up with a thug like Alex Brodey? It was a shame.

'Where did you get it from?' he whispered, staring at the oversized lapel badge on which was roughly printed, 'BAZ IS RUBBISH', all smeared now and filthy, unwearable.

'Where do you think? I found it on our assembly hall floor, this morning. I'm supposed to have handed it to the police.'

'Police?'

'I think you should have a look at this,' and Baz took the *Denning Spotlight*, the town's local daily newspaper, from his pocket. 'Unless you've seen it already,' and he unrolled it.

'No,' murmured Kev. 'I've not been to school. I think I've got flu.'

'Has Alex Brodey got flu too, then?' Baz said sarcastically. 'I bet you pounds to pennies he's not been to school either.'

Kev didn't answer, he was too busy reading the lead story in the *Spotlight*. 'Mystery Blaze at Top School', the headline screamed.

He turned white, and his hands flew up to his mouth, dropping the paper. 'Baz, I . . . God . . . this is terrible. We never meant, I mean . . . we *never* started a fire, *honest*. We just went in through the window and messed those stalls up a bit and then Alex went mad with his aerosol. *I* couldn't do anything. He was going crazy.'

'It *was* you, then?'

Kev had got to his feet, come over to Baz and was clutching feverishly at his shoulder. He really was frightened. 'Don't go to the police about us, Baz,' he pleaded. '*Please*, don't tell on us. My dad, he'd go spare, he's so depressed. He's applied for these millions of jobs like, and everybody says no. It's terrible. And the Brodeys . . . they're maniacs, they'd *kill* their Alex. God, I beg you Baz, I'll do anything, *anything*.' He was crying.

Baz found to his surprise that his arm was creeping round Kev's shivering shoulders. 'It's OK. I'm not going to say anything. Nobody got hurt, that's the point. I suppose it was Alex's cigarette. Was it?'

Kev nodded, 'Suppose so, but I'm *sure* it wasn't on purpose. We just went back through the window, when he'd, you know . . . '

'No one was injured, anyhow,' Baz repeated. 'It's just a bit of a mess. Really, I only came to give you your property back,' and he switched *Neighbours* on again, to cover their mutual embarrassment; but Harold and Madge were arguing, so he switched the sound off.

Kev hurled the badge into a corner and stared at the screen, glassy-eyed. His thin, pale body, still seemed to have the shakes.

'Your dad's still on the booze then?' Baz said, crumpling one of the lager cans. He got it quite flat too. That was good. His grip must be strengthening. Kev nodded. 'What does it look like? He's already at the Bay Horse. They never seem to shut these days, pubs. He's waiting to see if they'll give him a job at Sligo's on the new factory extension. It'd pay better than Ridgeways and he knows the foreman. But after that do out on the street, when the police turned up ... well ... I ask you, are they *likely* to give him a job?'

'See what you mean,' Baz said sympathetically.

'How's your election campaign gone, then?' Kev said, his voice not much above a whisper, but clearly wanting a change of subject. 'Never thought you'd go Green. They're just nutters, aren't they?'

'How did you know I'd gone Green?' Baz said, rather sharply. He sensed that between them, Kev and Alex Brodey knew more about Bryce's School election than anyone else in the town.

'Oh, you know. People were talking about it, on the bus like,' Kev said evasively.

'Well, I couldn't win on my own, but now I think it's a dead cert, and it's still happening, even though ... you know ... ' And he still felt proud, in spite of the wrecked stalls, the absence of one last big meeting, the head's repeated suggestions that he should stand down. He was going to *win* tomorrow, and only now did he know why he wanted to so desperately. He wanted to win for his father. In his generosity and bravery and compassion he'd been a real 'Common Man', the best.

'We *have* joined up,' he explained carefully, 'but it's my party.'

'And I'll cry if I want to,' said Kev sadly.

'What?' Baz didn't understand.

'"It's my party, and I'll cry if I want to." It's a song. My mum used to go around singing it, as a joke, like.' When Kev mentioned his mother though, it didn't feel like a 'joke' at all. Baz rather dreaded that he might start crying again.

'I go down for fish and chips for us on Thursdays,' he said briskly getting up. 'I could get you some, you could have them with me and my mum, in our house.'

Kev hesitated, obviously tempted. 'No thanks. I've had my tea. Anyhow, it's *Home and Away*.'

'Listen, you could watch that at ours. Go on. Don't be such a misery.'

'No. It's OK. You see, my dad might come back, and you know . . . I'd like to be in . . . '

Baz rolled up the *Spotlight* and tucked it inside his jacket. Then he retrieved the button badge from its greasy corner and slipped it into his pocket.

'What are you going to do with that?' asked Kev, suspicious again, obviously still unable to believe, quite, that Baz was going to keep his mouth shut. There was money on offer, for useful information, according to the *Spotlight*, and Baz was always broke, like him.

'It's going straight into the bin. They empty them in the morning, don't they?'

'Thanks, pal,' Kev whispered as he went through the back door, 'and listen, I'm not kidding, good luck tomorrow.'

17

Baz was late for school next day, because one of Mum's old people had had a fall in the night and he had to sit with her, while his mother tried to get the doctor. She knew it was election morning, but she said she couldn't leave poor Mrs Heggerty sprawled at the bottom of the stairs with what looked like a broken leg. In the end, when the doctor did show up, she gave him money for a taxi. This was almost unheard of in their house, but she seemed to know just how much the campaign had meant to him. He'd given her one of Alice's 'Vote for Baz' badges, and she was wearing it on her anorak.

When he got to school and started pulling his coat off, people were already filing into the gym for assembly. The Anderson Hall was still sealed off. He'd wanted to look extra smart this morning, for Slime's benefit, but he only just had time to relieve himself, and run a wet paper towel over his face, before joining the tail-end of 3M's queue, tagging on after Polly, who'd also only just arrived. He'd been on a spying mission, he said, and he looked grim.

'What's up?' Baz whispered, as they filtered into the gym. You weren't supposed to speak before assembly, and the prefects were watching.

'Jugsy has just stuck up a notice, about the voting. You know those "modifications" he kept going on about? Well, guess what? The *staff* are having a vote now, after all Slime said about it being a "school only" thing. I think that might affect the numbers and it's not fair . . . in fact, I shouldn't think it's actually *legal*.'

Baz shrugged. 'I don't think "legal" enters into it, does it? I mean Slime made the rules for this election, so I reckon he can break them, if he wants. Anyhow, who's going to vote for Julius Malin? Most of the staff are on our side, aren't they?'

Polly frowned and looked at a scrap of paper. '50/50 I'd say, with luck. But then there's Slime. He'll vote. It could be as close as that.'

'But you said we were ahead, Polly.'

'We *were*, but that was before they painted your name all over the hall, and wrecked the stalls.'

'But that wasn't *my* fault.'

'I know, but I've told you before, people are . . .'

'I know, I know,' interrupted Baz, '"people are fickle".'

'Pollitt . . . Bradshaw . . . Report to me at break, for disobedience marks, if you please,' Mr Bannerjee rapped from the front of the gym. 'You know quite well that there is absolutely *no* talking before assembly.'

Subsiding, Polly blew a very discreet raspberry at him; Baz couldn't even be bothered to do that.

Voting took place in the first lesson, and again at break, and the school morning was slightly shortened so that the results could be announced before lunch. It was all going to be very rushed, Baz noticed, only ten minutes for the big announcement, as if Slime, having decided to go ahead, was now running away from something, wanting to wash his hands of the affair just as quickly as possible.

They all questioned Jugsy during Form Business, but at first nobody could get anything out of him. 'You've seen the headmaster's notice,' he snapped. 'It's fairly clear, isn't it? Contrary to what we had all been expecting, the teachers, that is, the Senior Common Room, are allowed to take part in your election. I, however, will *not* be voting. On principle.'

'What principle, sir?' said Jake. You could always rely on him to put the awkward question that nobody else would dare to ask.

Jugsy looked as if he was going to turn away without

replying. Then he spoke. He was very quiet and very tense, almost on the brink of tears, Baz felt. 'If you must know, Elder, the principle of honesty. I have been against this election from the beginning, as you are aware, and everything I predicted has come true. We have had all kinds of silly, unseemly behaviour: rowdyism, vandalism, a fire ... Well, you *know* what's been happening. But the election has been run along certain lines, and now, on a whim, the headmaster has seen fit to change his tack. I'm not happy with that, and I would say so in public. I've never said a word against the way he runs his ship before, but I feel I have to say it now. I will not be voting this morning. Now, return to your place.'

Nobody wanted to talk after that. In the form-room emotion was thick, and feelings running high. Baz had a new vision of dry, shrivelled-up Jugsy now; he was a man of principle, a man of *honour*. Jugsy had flown bombers over Germany. He'd got medals.

Slime announced the results at top speed and in such a summary fashion, that they didn't really need the whole ten minutes. He simply got the candidates up on to the platform – only three now, Julius, Harriet and Baz – and announced the voting figures in ascending order. He tried to make a joke out of the last-minute Senior Common Room vote, but nobody actually laughed. Word had got round that he'd been 'cooking the books', that was Jake Elder's word for it, changing the basic rules at the very last minute. People were disgusted.

His point was that the teachers, had he only *thought*, should have been in on the voting from the very beginning. 'After all,' he said, with his broad mirthless smile, 'this election is all about fair play, about *equality*. Basil Bradshaw has reminded us of that most effectively. So now,' he went on, 'the vital figures: Harriet Weatherall, More Jelly – 117 votes. Very well done, Harriet. Basil Bradshaw, Common Man – 295 votes. Excellent show, Bradshaw,' and he initiated some hearty clapping. 'Julius Malin, Cut Above – 296 votes. So by *one* vote – and my goodness, what drama there was at the ballot-boxes this morning – I declare that Julius Malin, of Cut Above, is the outright winner.'

At the piano, after a curt nod from Slime, Granny Baxter immediately played the opening bars of a hymn and ended the rather feeble clapping, as the three candidates returned to their seats.

> 'He who would valiant be,
> 'Gainst all disaster . . .'

Under cover of the music, the whispering began. 'One vote,' Polly was raging. '*One* miserable vote. Malin got in because of that staff thing, and nobody had even heard of it until this morning!'

Baz stood there silently, trying to find hymn 503, but the page was too blurred. He couldn't read the words and it was his favourite hymn, too, it was about courage and strength; it was about Dad.

'Never mind, Baz,' Alice said, observing him very closely, and squeezing his arm. 'We all know you won *really*.' On the other side Vanessa pressed his hand silently, then whispered, 'I think you're *great*.'

Baz felt eyes on him and looked up to see Jugsy peering at him along the row. He was smiling faintly, seemed to be mouthing, 'Don't worry,' and awkwardly, unpractised, seemed too, to be offering some kind of 'thumbs up' signal, 1950s' style.

> 'No foes shall stay his might
> Though he with giants fight . . .'

The whole school was singing now, but Baz couldn't respond to Jugsy, nor sing with them. He was crying.

Instead of going to his extra hockey practice after school, he let the service bus leave without him, and walked all the way home. It was nearly three miles, but he didn't even notice. The way he was feeling he could have walked for ever and ever.

Those unexpected, embarrassing tears had been replaced by white-hot anger.

His mother was out. She'd gone up to the hospital to see Mrs Heggerty, but she'd left a note saying 'Congratulations!' She must mean the election, and that she'd thought he'd won. But it was no good Alice and people saying he'd 'won really'; Malin had come in with that extra point, that was the top and bottom of it. *He'd lost*; all because of Slime's dishonesty.

Up in his bedroom he stripped down to his boxer shorts, put on his jeans and a T-shirt and slipped home Mum's biggest ear-rings yet. He could do it without looking now, he'd got the knack. The whole of his Bryce's uniform he stuffed into a plastic bin-liner, blazer, tie, non-regulation shoes, the lot. Then he marched downstairs and rammed it into the dustbin. After that he felt better.

Coming back into the house, he caught sight of his 'acceptance' letter from Bryce's. Mum was proud of it. She'd had it framed, and it hung over the sideboard. He grabbed it and raised his knee, determined to smash it to smithereens. Then he caught Dad's eye, staring out at him from the Lake District photo, and Mum looking so pretty and young, so . . . *hopeful*. He musn't smash it, however angry he felt about Bryce's. She wouldn't understand. So he put it back, letting it swing on its nail. Perhaps he could persuade her to put it in a drawer. He wasn't at all sure he wanted to go back to that school ever again.

For something to do he switched on the television and went channel-hopping. Two Australian soap operas, the schools Maths programme and a ludicrous phone-in about biological washing-powders. He switched off in disgust, wondering what telly-addict Kev found to watch all the time. He wasn't watching at the moment, though. Through the back door which had swung open, Baz could hear a radio blaring in next door's yard. He'd be out there, tinkering with his bike most likely.

Baz got over via the dustbins and said, 'Hello.'

'Hi,' said Kev, very cheerfully, 'how are you doing?'

'OK. What about you?'

Kev suddenly came to life. 'Great. You know Dad? Well he *wasn't* at the Bay Horse last night, he was at Sligo's. And, listen to this, they've given him a job. It's *miles* better than what he was doing at Ridgeways. So, if I can sell this wreck, he says I can have a new bike next month. Isn't it great?'

'Great,' Baz echoed, flat as a pancake.

'What's up with you, then?' Kev said, staring at him and chucking down his spanner. 'You did *win*, didn't you? I missed the bus home. What happened?'

'We lost. By one measly vote.'

Kev stretched an arm out and squeezed his shoulder. 'Aw, that's rotten, Baz, after all you did . . .'

'Changed the rules, didn't they? At the last minute the head said the staff could have a vote, too. But it was a lie really, he just made it up, it wasn't in the rules of the election, not at the beginning it wasn't. No, he just wanted me out of it. My face doesn't fit at Bryce's, Kev.'

'But you got that scholarship. You got the *top* scholarship . . .'

'He didn't like what I was saying, mate, it's as simple as that. Since I went on telly reporters have been up to the school, radio people, all sorts. He doesn't *want* someone like me standing for the school, someone with new ideas. He says I'm "subversive" or something. That's what Matron told me anyhow. You see, Julius Malin's no threat, that's why he had to win. It's just, you know, "more of the same", with him.'

Kev said, slowly and with great embarrassment, 'You could have told them about us, Baz, about me and Alex. Would he have tried to get rid of you then, do you think?'

'Well, I wasn't going to do *that*, now was I?' Baz said fiercely. 'You're my mate.'

Baz told Kev that he might never go back to Bryce's. Hadn't he just shoved his uniform in the bin? Instead he got his bike out and they went up on to Darnley Moor. He used to go up there every Sunday with Dad, while Mum had a sleep.

Darnley-in-Makerfield was an ugly little town, with all its factories and railway lines and cooling towers. But from up here, on this golden autumn day, it looked marvellous. They pushed their bikes as far as Summit View, chucked the machines on the grass, then just stood and stared.

On the way up Baz had told Kev about his new view of Jugsy. 'He's disgusted now,' he said, 'according to The Cow, Matron that is. He wouldn't vote, and he's thinking of retiring early. That's what people are saying, anyhow.'

'Thought he was brain-dead,' said Kev, chewing on some grass.

'He *is*, but honestly, he's OK. He flew bombers in the war.' Baz wouldn't ever forget how he'd peered anxiously along the row in assembly. How he'd tried to be 'with it' and do the thumbs-up sign.

'I don't think you should leave Bryce's, Baz, I don't really,' said Kev, still chewing steadily.

'Why not? I bet *you'd* want to leave. All that effort for the election, and we were winning, mate. Then Slime just invents a new rule, because he's frightened about the school's reputation. It makes me sick. I've told you, they don't approve of what I *stand* for.'

'But look at it this way,' Kev argued, 'if you *did* leave, then nothing would ever change, would it? You spoke out, Baz, for fairness, for equal rights. People listened to you. OK, so you didn't win this time, but if you left, well *they'd* have won, wouldn't they?'

There was a very long silence, and Baz looked at the view. The gentle green hills, furred with golden, burning trees, in the cleft of the valley where the stream ran; the high, bright sky, and a gentle sun lighting up the leaves as the breeze ruffled through, turning pale sides to dark.

'I dunno. S'pose so. I don't know what I think any more.'

'I do,' said Kev. '*This* is what I think.' Unpinning the 'Vote for Baz' badge from his friend's denim jacket, he fastened it on to his own and tapped it proudly. 'That's what I think,' he repeated shyly.

Baz smiled a little smile and, together, they began to wheel their bikes back down the hill.

FLOWER OF JET

Bel Mooney

It's the time of the miners' strike. Tom Farrell's father is branded with the word Tom most dreads; Melanie Wall's father is the strike leader. How can Tom and Melanie's friendship survive the violence and bitterness of both sides? Things are to grow far worse than they ever imagined, for Melanie and Tom discover a treacherous plot that could destroy both their families. And they have to act fast if they're going to stop it.

MIGHTIER THAN THE SWORD

Clare Bevan

Adam had always felt he was somehow special, different from the rest of the family, but could he really be a modern-day King Arthur, the legendary figure they're learning about at school? Inspired by the stories they are hearing in class, Adam and his friends become absorbed in a complex game of knights and good deeds. All they need is a worthy cause for which to fight. So when they discover that the local pond is under threat, Adam's knights are ready to join battle with the developers.

Reality and legend begin to blur in this lively, original story about an imaginative boy who doesn't let a mere wheelchair get in his way of adventure.

AGAINST THE STORM

Gaye Hicyilmaz

'As Mehmet is drawn into his parents' ill-considered scheme to go and live in Ankara, the directness and the acute observation of Gaye Hicyilmaz carry the reader with him ... Terrible things happen: illness, humiliation, death. But Mehmet is a survivor, and as the book closes, "a sort of justice" has been done, and a satisfying victory achieved. It is a sort of justice too ... that in all the dire traffic of unpublishable manuscripts something as fresh and powerful as this should emerge' – *The Times*

JEALOUS JOOLS AND DOMINIQUE

Sam McBratney

Many are the obstacles in the path of Jools's love for Dominique. Not least is Valroy, 'an alloy of several metals' and an interfering robot if ever there was one. The damage looks irreparable until Jools's eccentric Uncle Jerome steps in with some technical help.

ADAM'S ARK

Paul Stewart

Oscar's arrival in the house has a dramatic effect on Adam. In discovering that he can think-talk with the cat, he is at last able to make contact with the world around him. But the more he learns about the sad plight of animals everywhere, the more determined he is to discover why he alone has this extraordinary ability to communicate with them.

THE FRIENDSHIP AND OTHER STORIES

Mildred D. Taylor

In the Mississippi of the 1930s, Cassie Logan and her brothers have to watch their mouths when white folks are around. So when old Mr Tom Bee, a former slave, dares to call a white store-keeper by his first name, the children are expecting trouble. But even they are not prepared for the brutal scenes which they are to witness on that hot summer afternoon.